Lilly squared her shoulders and pulled in a deep breath as Riccardo stopped in front of them. He leaned down and brushed a kiss against her cheek. "Late and wearing pink. One would think you're deliberately trying to antagonize me, Lilly."

Her pulse sped into overdrive. "Maybe I'm celebrating my newfound freedom."

"Ah, but you don't have it yet," he countered, moving his lips to the other cheek. "And you aren't putting me in the kind of mood to grant it to you."

Lilly was aware of the eyes on them as he pulled back and stung her face with a reprimanding look that made her feel like a fifth-grader. "Don't play games with me, Riccardo," she said quietly. "I will turn around and walk out of here so fast you won't know what hit you."

His dark eyes glinted, his mouth tipped up at the corners. "You've already done that, *tesoro*, and now you're back."

All about the author...
Jennifer Hayward

JENNIFER HAYWARD has been a fan of romance and adventure since filching her sister's Harlequin Presents novels to escape her teenage angst.

Jennifer penned her first romance at nineteen. When it was rejected, she bristled at her mother's suggestion that she needed more life experience. She went on to complete a journalism degree before settling into a career in public relations. Years of working alongside powerful, charismatic CEOs and traveling the world provided perfect fodder for the arrogant alpha males she loves to write about.

With a suitable amount of life experience under her belt, she sat down and conjured up the sexiest, most delicious Italian wine magnate she could imagine, had him make his biggest mistake, and gave him a wife on the run. That story, *The Divorce Party*, won her Harlequin's So You Think You Can Write contest and a book contract. Turns out, Mother knew best.

A native of Canada's gorgeous East Coast, Jennifer now lives in Toronto with her Viking husband and their young Viking-in-training. She considers her ten-year-old-strong book club, composed of some of the most amazing women she's ever met, a sacrosanct date in her calendar. And someday, they will have their monthly meeting at her fantasy beach house, waves lapping at their feet, wineglasses in hand.

You can find Jennifer on Facebook and Twitter.

This is Jennifer's stunning debut—we hope you love it as much as we do!

Did you know this is also available as an ebook?

Jennifer Hayward

The Divorce Party

HARLEQUIN PRESENTS®

Recycling programs
for this product may
not exist in your area.

ISBN-13: 978-0-373-13189-1

THE DIVORCE PARTY

Copyright © 2013 by Jennifer Drogell

All rights reserved. Except for use in any review, the reproduction or utilization of this work in whole or in part in any form by any electronic, mechanical or other means, now known or hereafter invented, including xerography, photocopying and recording, or in any information storage or retrieval system, is forbidden without the written permission of the publisher, Harlequin Enterprises Limited, 225 Duncan Mill Road, Don Mills, Ontario M3B 3K9, Canada.

This is a work of fiction. Names, characters, places and incidents are either the product of the author's imagination or are used fictitiously, and any resemblance to actual persons, living or dead, business establishments, events or locales is entirely coincidental.

This edition published by arrangement with Harlequin Books S.A.

For questions and comments about the quality of this book, please contact us at CustomerService@Harlequin.com.

® and TM are trademarks of Harlequin Enterprises Limited or its corporate affiliates. Trademarks indicated with ® are registered in the United States Patent and Trademark Office, the Canadian Trade Marks Office and in other countries.

Printed in U.S.A.

Dear Reader,

This story begins on a cold winter day with a cup of coffee, a newspaper and a real-life party that sparked a tale that just had to be told.

On the front page of my newspaper that morning was the story of a lavish divorce party a Manhattan billionaire was throwing to celebrate the end of his three-year marriage. The embossed invitations, the incredibly civilized approach to the end of a union due to irreconcilable differences fascinated me. What would bring a couple to this point? Why would anyone want to end their marriage in front of family and friends?

I started to wonder—what if the billionaire didn't really want a divorce? What if what he really wanted was his wife back and this was the only way he could get her in the same room with him? What if they were madly in love but the very act of being together destroyed them? Could this marriage ever be saved?

My billionare became sexy Italian wine magnate, Riccardo De Campo, and his feisty, on-the-run wife, Lilly.

I've dreamed of writing romances for as long as I can remember, but the story of Riccardo and Lilly's tempestuous relationship was special. It got me out of bed one night to write the first chapter while I was knee deep in another book and wouldn't let me go until I'd written 'the end'.

I entered Riccardo and Lilly's story, *The Divorce Party,* in Harlequin's 2012 So You Think You Can Write contest hoping others would love it as much as I did. Never dreaming the De Campos would capture the imagination of so many people and win me the publishing contract I've always wanted. Every minute of that journey was magical.

I've had a hard time letting Riccardo and Lilly go. I hope you do too.

Enjoy!

Jennifer

I'd love to hear from you! I can be reached at www.jenniferhaywardromance.com or on Twitter - jenhayward_.

"Was that a whale?" Zimsky asked.

"Nope," Josh said. He showed no sign of any kind of collision on his board at all. "Depth?"

"Sixteen hundred feet," Beck said.

"Hull integrity is still good," Serge said.

"You sure?" Josh asked as another shudder ran through the ship.

"Increase the impeller speed," Brazzleton said. "We're going to need additional control."

"Done," Iverson said.

"What was it?" Josh asked, not wanting to take his eyes off of his panel.

"An underwater earthquake," Stickley said from Deep-Earth Control back in Utah. "A good-sized one."

Another shudder ran through the craft, this time harder and more destructive than the last two.

"Four thousand feet," Beck reported.

"We're losing steering," Iverson said.

Of that Josh had no doubt. On the screen in front of them it was clear that they were now caught in some massive underwater whirlpool, more than likely set off by the earthquakes.

And it was tossing them at the rock wall of the Trench.

CHAPTER ONE

IT WAS GOING to be bad.

Lilly Anderson winced and put a hand to her pounding head. If she held herself in just that position, with the pressure building in her head like the vicious storms that picked up intensity across the plains of the midwest, it might not become a full-on migraine.

Might not.

Except staying in the dim confines of Riccardo's Rolls-Royce, driven by his long-time driver Tony, wasn't an option tonight. She was late for her own divorce party. Excessively late for the one thing that would give her what she wanted above all else. Her freedom from her husband.

"Oh, my God."

Her twin sister Alex made a sound low in her throat. "How can they print this stuff?"

"What?"

"Nothing."

"Alex, read it to me."

"It's Jay Kaiken's column. You don't want me to."

"Read it."

"Okay, but I warned you." She cleared her throat. "In what's expected to be the most scandalous, juiciest, talked-about water cooler event of the season, billionaire wine magnate Riccardo De Campo and former Iowa farmgirl-turned-sports-physiotherapist Lilly De Campo host their divorce party tonight. I once suggested they were the only passionately in love couple left in New York. But apparently even that fairytale doesn't actually exist. Rumors of heartthrob Riccardo's infidelity surfaced and this once solid marriage ended up in the toilet. So it's with mixed feelings that I bid this partnership adieu tonight. I have the invite and will bring you all the salacious details."

She crumpled up the tabloid and threw it on the floor. "He's such an SOB."

Lilly closed her eyes, a fresh wave of nausea rolling over her. No matter how many times she'd envisioned this moment, this freedom from Riccardo, she had never envisioned this. Nor the insanely mixed feelings she had right about now.

"Sorry, Lil. I shouldn't have started on those."

"You're a PR person, Alex. You're addicted."

"Still, I suck. I'm really sorry."

Lilly smoothed her fuchsia silk dress over her knees. It was elegant enough—and in Riccardo's most hated color, which was an added bonus—but it felt as if it was clinging in all the wrong places. A glance in the mirror before they'd left had told her she was paper-white, with dark bags under her hazel eyes. Haunted. In fact the only thing that *was* right was her hair, blowdried to glossy, straight perfection by her savior of a stylist.

It was a problem—this not feeling together. She felt she was already at a disadvantage. Facing Riccardo without her mask, without all her defences in place, was never a good way to start.

"You look a little too good," Alex murmured. "I think you should have put something frumpier on. And maybe messed your hair up a bit."

Lilly took the compliment and felt a bit better. Her sister was, if nothing else, the bluntest person she'd ever met. "Now, why would I do that?"

"Because Riccardo is like a banned substance for you,"

her sister said drily. "And your marriage almost destroyed you. Be ugly, Lilly, it's the easiest way."

Lilly smiled, then winced as her head did another inside-out throb. "He's finally agreed to give me the divorce. You should be doing a happy dance."

"If I thought he was giving in I might be. Has he given you the papers yet?"

"I'm hoping he'll do that tonight."

Alex scowled. "It's not like him to do this. He's up to something."

Her heart dropped about a thousand feet. "Maybe he's decided it's time to replace me."

"One can only hope."

A stab of pain lanced through her. She should be elated Riccardo had finally seen the light. Seen that there was no way they could ever reconcile after everything that had happened. So why had his decree that they finally end this with an official public announcement hit her with the force of an eighteen-wheeler? She certainly hadn't been pining away the past twelve months, hoping his refusal to divorce her meant he still loved her. And there was no way she'd harbored any silly notions that he was going to come climbing through her window and carry her back home, like in some Hollywood movie, with a promise to do everything differently.

That would have been stupid and naive.

She squared her shoulders. He likely did have another prospect in mind. Everything Riccardo did was a means to an end.

"If I ever want to be free to pursue a real relationship with Harry I need Riccardo's signature on that piece of paper."

"Oh, come on, Lil." Her sister's beautiful face twisted in a grimace. "Harry Taylor might be a decorated cardiothoracic surgeon, Doctors Without Borders and all that lovely stuff, but *really?* He's dull as dishwater. You might as well marry him and move back to Mason Hill."

"He's also handsome, smart and sweet," Lilly defended tartly, not needing to tell her sister there wasn't a hope in hell of her moving back to the miserable existence they'd escaped at eighteen. "I'm lucky to have him."

Alex waved a hand at her. "You can't tell me after Riccardo he doesn't seem like some watered-down version—like grape juice instead of Cabernet."

"You just told me Riccardo was bad news for me."

"So is Harry Taylor. He'll bore you to death."

Lilly had to steel herself not to laugh out loud, because that just would have hurt too much. "I'm through with men who make my heart pound and my palms go sweaty. It's self-destructive for me."

"The particular one you picked might have been... What time were we supposed to have been there, by the way?"

Lilly checked her watch. "A half-hour ago."

Alex gave her a wicked smile. "Riccardo's going to love that."

She squirmed in her seat. She was always late. No matter how hard she tried. Because it was just in her nature to try and squeeze too much into the day, and also because her multi-million-dollar athletes kept waltzing in half an hour late. But Riccardo had never seemed to care what the reason was. He wanted what he wanted when he wanted it. And that was all.

Alex's expression shifted. "I talked to David today."

Lilly froze. Alex talking to their brother back in Iowa only meant one thing. "How's Lisbeth?"

Alex frowned. "He said she had a really bad week. The doctor is saying she needs that experimental treatment within the next few months if it's going to do any good."

Dammit. Lilly twisted her hands together in her lap, feeling that familiar blanket of hopelessness settle over her. Her youngest sister Lisbeth had leukemia. She'd been told three months ago she was out of remission, and her doctor was advocating a ground-breaking new treatment as the one thing that might give her a fighting chance. But the treatment cost a fortune.

"I can't ask Riccardo for the money, Alex. I know it's crazy, but I can't give him that kind of power over me."

"I know." Alex put her hand over hers and squeezed. "We'll figure it out. There has to be a way."

Lilly pursed her lips. "I'm going to go back to the bank tomorrow. Maybe they'll let me do it in installments."

There had to be a way. Lisbeth *had* to get that treatment. Tonight, however, she had to focus on survival.

Her hands shook in her lap and her head throbbed like a jackhammer as they turned down a leafy, prestigious street toward the De Campo townhouse. She had taken one look at the beautiful old limestone mansion and fallen in love. Riccardo had taken one look at her face and bought it for her. "You love it," he'd said, not even blinking at the thirty-five-million-dollar price tag. "We'll buy it."

They swung to a halt in front of the home she'd run out of with only a suitcase twelve months ago, when she'd finally had the guts to leave him. It was the first time she'd been back and it occurred to her she was truly crazy making that time tonight. Divorce parties might be in vogue, but did she really want to detonate her and Riccardo's relationship in front of all the people who'd made her life miserable?

She didn't have a choice. She scooted over as Tony came around to open the door. Riccardo had been adamant. *"We need to end this standoff,"* he'd said. *"We need to make the state of our relationship official. Be there, Lilly, or this isn't happening."*

She forced herself to grasp Tony's hand. But her legs didn't seem to recognize the need to function as she stepped out of the car on trembling limbs that wanted to cave beneath her. The long, snakelike line of limousines made her suck in a breath. The memory of Riccardo sweeping her out of this car the night of their first anniversary and carrying her upstairs made it catch in her throat. He had made love to her with an intensity that night that had promised he would love her forever.

The images of the beginning and the end collided together in an almost blinding reminder of how quickly things could turn bad.

How hearts could be shattered.

"We can still turn around," her sister said quietly, coming to stand by her side. "If Riccardo really wants this divorce he'll come to you."

No, he wouldn't. Lilly shook her head. "I need to do this."

Do this and you won't ever have to live in a world you don't belong in again.

She walked woodenly up the front path alongside Alex. A dark-haired young man in a catering uniform opened the door and ushered them inside.

"How weird to have someone invite you into your own home," Alex whispered.

"It's not my home anymore."

But everything about it was. She couldn't help but stare up at the one-of-a-kind Italian cut-glass chandelier that was the centerpiece of the entryway. She and Riccardo had chosen it together on their honeymoon in the little town of Murano, famous for its glass. They had hand-picked a crystal to have their initials carved into, which had been placed on the bottom row. Riccardo had insisted on adding two entwined hearts beside their initials.

"It symbolizes us," he'd said. "We're no longer two separate people—we are one."

She lurched on her high heels, feeling whatever composure she'd had disintegrate. The urge to run far away from here as fast as she could was so overwhelming she could barely keep her feet planted on the floor.

"Lilly…" Alex murmured worriedly, her gaze on her face.

"I'm okay." She forced herself to smile at the young man offering to show them up the staircase to the ballroom. "We know the way."

She climbed the gleaming wooden staircase alongside Alex, her heartbeat accelerating with every step she took. By the time they'd reached the top of the stairs and turned toward the glimmering ballroom it was in her mouth.

You can do this. You've done this hundreds of times before.

Except Riccardo had been by her side then. A rock in a world that had never been hers. And tonight was the beginning of LAR—Life After Riccardo.

She paused at the entrance, taking in the glittering colors and jewels of the beautifully dressed crowd, set off by the muted glow of a dozen priceless antique chandeliers that dated back to the English Regency period. A jazz band played in the corner of the room, but the buzz of a hundred conversations rose above it.

Her back stiffened. She hated jazz. Was Riccardo trying to make a statement? To illustrate to her how he'd moved on?

Alex grabbed her arm and propelled her forward. "You need a drink."

Or ten, Lilly thought grimly as dozens of curious gazes turned on them and a buzz ran through the crowd. She switched herself on to autopilot—the only way she knew how to function in a situation like this—and started walking.

She lifted her chin when she saw Jay Kaiken and kept walking. As they moved toward the bar at the back of the room the strangest thing happened. Like the parting of the Red Sea, the crowd moved aside, dividing down the center of the room. On her left she recognized friends and acquaintances who had chosen to keep in touch with her rather than Riccardo after their separation. On her right she saw Riccardo's business associates, his brother, cousins and political contacts.

"It's like our wedding all over again," she breathed, remembering how she'd walked into that beautiful old Catholic cathedral on the Upper East Side to find her family and friends on one side—the neatly dressed, less-than-glamorous Iowa farm contingent alongside her girlfriends and schoolmates—and Riccardo's much larger, understatedly elegant clan on the other—all ancient bloodlines and aristocratic heritage.

As if their marriage was to be divided from the beginning.

Maybe that should have been her first clue.

She held her head high and kept walking. A tingle went down her spine. Her skin went cold. Riccardo was in the room. Watching her. She could feel it.

Turning her head, she found him—like a homing pigeon seeking its target. He looked furious. Seething. She swallowed hard, a flock of butterflies racing through her stomach. Riccardo spoke four languages—English, Spanish, German and his native Italian. But he did not have to utter a single word from those sensuous, dangerous lips for her to understand the emotion radiating from his eyes.

Hell. She touched her face in a nervous gesture that drew his gaze. Only Riccardo had ever been able to pull off that passionate intensity while still calling himself a twentieth-century man.

"Don't let him intimidate you," Alex murmured. "This is your divorce party, remember? Own it."

Easier in theory than in practice. Particularly so when Riccardo relieved a waiter of two glasses of champagne and strode toward them, with a look of intent on his face that shook her to her core. She absorbed this new Riccardo. He looked as indecently gorgeous as ever in a black tux that set off his dark good looks. But it was the hard edge to him that was different. The strongly carved lines of his face seemed to have deepened, harshened. He'd shaved off the thick, dark waves that had used to fall over his forehead in favor of a short buzz cut that made him look tougher, even more dangerously attractive if that was possible. And the ruthless expession on his face, the glitter in those dark eyes, had never been used on her quite like that before.

Her tongue cleaved to the roof of her mouth, her pulse picking up into a rapid, insistent rhythm that had her nails digging into her palms. Why, after everything they'd gone through, was he still the only man who could simply look at her and make her shake in her shoes?

Alex nudged her. "Dangerous controlled substance, remember?"

Lilly squared her shoulders and pulled in a deep breath as Riccardo stopped in front of them. He leaned down and brushed a kiss against her cheek. "Late and wearing pink. One would think you're deliberately trying to antagonize me, Lilly."

Her pulse sped into overdrive. "Maybe I'm celebrating my new-found freedom."

"Ah, but you don't have it yet," he countered, moving his lips to the other cheek. "And you aren't putting me in the kind of mood to grant it to you."

Lilly was aware of all the eyes on them as he pulled back and stung her face with a reprimanding look that made her feel like a fifth-grader. "Don't play games with me, Riccardo," she said quietly. "I will turn around and walk out of here so fast you won't know what hit you."

His dark eyes glinted. His mouth tipped up at the corners. "You've already done that, *tesoro,* and now you're back."

Something exploded in her head. She was about to tell him exactly what she thought of his ultimatum, but he was bending down and kissing Alex.

"*Buonasera.* I trust you're well?"

"Never better," Alex muttered.

"Do you think I might have a word with my wife alone?"

Wife. He'd said the word with such supreme confidence—a statement of fact that hung on the air between them like a challenge. A tremor went down Lilly's spine.

"Whatever you have to say you can say it in front of my sister."

"Not *this.*" His gaze bored into hers. "Unless you want every gossip columnist in New York reporting on our conversation, I suggest we do it in private."

Considering it was only in the last few months Lilly's name had finally *disappeared* from those columns, she conceded that might be a good idea. "Fine."

Riccardo turned to Alex. "Gabe is getting you a drink at the bar."

Alex rolled her eyes. "Determined to force a confrontation between all the members of the De Campo and Anderson families tonight?"

"You're only antagonistic toward the people who evoke strong emotions in you," Riccardo taunted. "Try not to rip him in two, will you?"

"You think that's a good idea?" Lilly murmured, more to distract herself from the warm pressure of Riccardo's big hand splayed against her back as he directed her from the room than out of concern for her sister, who could hold her own.

"They love baiting each other. It'll be the highlight of their evening."

She struggled to keep up with his long strides as he walked her up the stairs to the third floor, where the bedrooms were, nodding at the security guard stationed there. "Why are we coming up here?" she murmured, flushing at the guard's interested gaze. "Why don't we just talk in your study?"

He kept walking past the guest bedrooms toward the

master suite. "I won't risk being overheard. We'll talk on the patio off our bedroom."

"*Your* bedroom," Lilly corrected. "And I don't think—"

"*Basta,* Lilly." He glared at her. "I'm your husband, not some guy trying to come on to you."

Lilly clamped her mouth shut and followed him through the double doors of the master suite. She would not, whatever she did, look at the huge canopy bed they had shared. The scene of more erotically charged encounters than she cared to remember.

Their marriage bed. The place where she and Riccardo had always been able to communicate.

He pushed open the French doors to the large patio. The rose bushes he'd had planted for her along the edge had already started to bloom, emitting the gorgeous perfume she'd always loved.

Ugh. She shoved her sentimentality down with a determined effort and spun to face him.

"So?" she prompted, hostility edging her words. "What is it you have to say?"

His gaze darkened. "You're not too big for me to put you over my knee, *tesoro.* Push me a little harder and I will."

Lilly's cheeks burned at that very seductive image. To her horror, her mind took her there—took her to a vision of Riccardo holding her over his muscular thighs, her naked behind squirming as he brought his hand down in a stinging reprimand.

Dear God.

A satisfied expression crossed his face. "Unnerving, isn't it, that we only have to speak to each other in a certain way and that happens?"

"*Damn you,* Riccardo." She planted her feet wide and faced him head-on. "For over a year I've been trying to get you to give me a divorce and you've flatly denied it. Then you call me out of the blue with this crazy idea of making it official with a party, and now you're playing cat and mouse with me. What the hell are you playing at?"

He crossed his arms over his chest and leaned back against the railing. "Maybe if you'd agreed to see me I wouldn't have resorted to this."

"Nothing good ever comes of us being together. You know that."

His eyes glimmered as they swept over her. "That's a big fat lie and you know it."

She wrapped her arms around herself. "Sex is not a good basis for a marriage."

"We had more than sex, Lilly." His deep voice softened, taking on those velvet undertones that could make her melt in a nanosecond. "We had way, way more than that."

"It wasn't enough! Do you know how happy I've been this past year?"

He paled beneath his deep tan. "*We* were happy once."

She hugged her arms tighter around herself and fought the ache in her chest that threatened to consume her. "We're better off apart and you know it."

"I will never agree to that."

She lifted her chin. "I want a divorce. And if you won't give it to me I'll have my lawyer fight you until you do."

His mouth flattened. "I will drag it out for years."

"Why?" She pushed her hair out of her face and gave him a desperate look. "We're done. We've hurt each other enough for a lifetime. We need to move on with our lives."

He jammed his hands into his pockets. The fierce, fighting expression in his eyes was one she knew all too well. But he said nothing. Silence sceamed between them until she thought she'd jump out of her skin.

"All right."

She stared at him. "All right what?"

"I will give you the divorce. On one condition."

She knew she should leave now—get the hell out of here as fast as she could. But she couldn't force her feet to move.

"I need you to remain my wife for six more months."

Her jaw dropped open. "Wh-what?"

"My father feels I need to present a more grounded image to the board before they make their decision on a CEO." He lifted his shoulders and twisted his lips in a cynical smile. "They apparently still haven't bought my reformed image."

Lilly came crashing back to earth with the force of a meteorite bent on destruction. Any illusions she'd harbored—and she realized now she *had* harbored a few—about Riccardo not wanting to divorce her because he still loved her vanished at the point of impact. Something hot and bright burned the back of her eyes.

"That's ridiculous," she managed huskily. "You left racing three years ago."

He shrugged. "It is what it is. I can't change their perception."

Lilly almost choked on the irony of it. Everything Riccardo had ever done when they were together had been to dispel the image of himself as a reckless young racecar driver who hadn't been committed to the family business.

She shook her head. "Our *marriage* fell apart because of your obsession with your job. Your single-minded fixation on becoming CEO."

"One of any number of issues our marriage had," he corrected grimly. "Be that as it may, my father wants us back togther. He thinks the media coverage will go a long way toward stabilizing my image with the board, and he's made it a condition in my having his support."

His father wanted her back in his life? She'd always believed Antonio De Campo had thought her far beneath his son, with her poor upbringing, but he had been too polite to say it.

"My father thinks you're a good influence on me." He gave a wry half-smile that softened those newly hardened features of his. "He's quite likely right about that."

"This is crazy." Lillly shook her head and paced to the opposite end of the patio. "We aren't even *capable* of pretending we're a happily married couple."

"You have a short memory, Lilly."

His soft reprimand drew her gaze to his face.

"Six months. That's all I'm asking."

"I want a divorce," she repeated, raising her voice as this insane conversation kept plowing forward. "What makes you think I would ever consider helping you?"

He tilted his head to one side. "What are you afraid of? That we have way more unfinished business than you care to admit?"

She squared her shoulders. "We are over, Riccardo. And this is not a good idea."

"It's a great idea. Six months buys you your freedom."

"What other conditions has your father imposed?" she asked helplessly. "Are you to stop driving fast cars and dating international supermodels?"

He scowled. "Not one of those rumors are true. There's been no one since you."

She stiffened. "We all know there's truth to the tabloids."

"Not one, Lilly."

"*Riccardo,*" she said desperately. "No."

He stalked over, invading her space. "What is it, *tesoro?* Got plans with Harry Taylor?"

How did he know about Harry? They'd been so low-key as to be socially non-existent. "Yes," she snapped. "I'd like to move on, and maybe you should do the same."

He lifted his hand and took her chin in his fingers. "You forget we made a vow, *amore mio.* 'For richer and poorer, in sickness and in health…'"

"That was before you broke it."

A dangerous glimmer entered his eyes. "I never slept with Chelsea Tate. We've had this conversation."

"We are never going to agree on *that,*" she bit out, throwing his words back at him. "Nor could we ever fake any real affection for each other. It would be laughable."

"Oh, but I think we could," he murmured, lowering his head to hers. "Even the thought of me spanking you turns you on."

She pulled out of his grip. "Riccardo—"

He slid a hand into her hair and brought her back. "You went there, Lilly. And so did I."

"No, I—"

He smothered her reply with a kiss Lilly felt down to her toes, deep and sensuous. He didn't bother with the preliminaries. He simply took—kissing her exactly the way he knew she liked it, using every weapon at his disposal. Lilly curled her fingers into his shirt, intending to push him away, but she didn't quite seem to be able to do it.

He pulled her closer, anchored her against him. "Ric—" she murmured as he changed angles and came back to her.

"Shut up, Lilly," he commanded, sliding his fingers up her bare arms and closing his mouth over hers.

This time his kiss was softer, more persuasive than controlling, pleasurable rather than punishing. And something fell apart inside her. It had been too long since he'd kissed her like this, too long since she'd been in his arms, and God help her...of all the things they had *not* been good at, it hadn't been this.

"Dammit." She grabbed a handful of shirt to steady herself. "This is not fair."

He slid a hand down over the curve of her hip and brought her body into full contact with his. The feel of his hard body against her made her shiver, remembering everything.

"Nothing was ever fair between us. It was like a wild rollercoaster ride we couldn't get enough of."

He shifted her between the hard muscles of his thighs and brought his mouth down on hers again with a look of pure intent. His rigid, pulsing arousal pressed against her, making Lilly ache all over.

No, an inner voice warned. But all that came out was a groan.

He dragged her even closer, a satisfied growl escaping his throat. "Open your mouth, Lil."

Caught up in the pure, hot sexual power he had over her, she obeyed. She didn't think about the one hundred and fifty people downstairs, or even what a huge mistake this was. She just wanted this kiss, this magic, the hot intimacy of his tongue tangling with hers.

Oh. She melted into him as her knees threatened to give way. It was like someone offering an alcoholic a double shot after months of abstinence. Pure hedonism. And she wrapped herself in it.

A flash of light exploded around them. She stumbled backward, disoriented, blinking into the bright light that kept coming and coming.

Riccardo cursed and pulled her away from the railing. "*Dio.* How did they get here?"

"A photographer?" Lilly asked dazedly.

He nodded.

She touched her fingers to her mouth, still burning from his kiss. Riccardo had security everywhere. It didn't make sense that a photographer would be able to get up here. "You planned that," she said flatly. "You set that up for your father's benefit."

"I set this party up for my father's benefit," he agreed darkly. "For the board's benefit. Not that photo."

She pressed her palms to her temples. She didn't want to be back here. She couldn't go on walking around like a half-alive person, going through the motions but never really feeling anything. She needed this divorce.

His face tightened. "What? Afraid the good doctor won't understand a six-month hiatus?"

She shook her head. "The answer is no. No, no and no."

He straighened his shirt and raked a hand through his hair. "We'll make the announcement at ten."

She turned her back on him and started for the door.

"I'll give you the house."

She stopped in her tracks.

"You've never wanted anything from me, but I know you love this house. I'll sign it over to you at the end of the six months."

Lilly opened her mouth to tell him where he could put his offer, but the words died in her mouth. The house would pay for Lisbeth's treatment. Fifty times over.

"Tempting, isn't it? Your dream house...without me in it?"

She counted to five before she turned around. As if any amount of money would be enough to convince her that revisitng their ruin of a marriage was worth it.

But she was desperate. And she didn't have the luxury of time.

She lifted her gaze to his. "I will think about it."

"Ten o'clock, Lilly." His smile didn't quite reach his eyes. "Think of yourself as Cinderella, only your deadline isn't midnight—it's ten. And I'm the devil you know."

CHAPTER TWO

LILLY SPENT THE intervening hours coming up with a million different reasons why she would be crazy to agree to Riccardo's proposal. He was once again using her in his single-minded pursuit of the De Campo CEO job. He didn't really want her—he wanted Lilly De Campo the figurehead, his perfect society wife who could smile and say intelligent things to the very intelligent people they met. And, dammit, her life was finally back on track! She had built up her practice, she had started to do the things she loved again, and she had a life.

Whether or not she was just going through the motions was irrelevant. She had been moving on.

Until that kiss tonight.

She touched her fingers to her mouth and tightness seized her chest. How could she kiss Riccardo like that when the same from Harry inspired only lukewarm affection?

"Which do you prefer, Lilly? Snakeskin or alligator?"

She gave the trendy young shoe designer who had cornered her and Alex a blank look. "Sorry?"

"I was asking if you prefer snakeskin or alligator… If I'd known you were doing this tonight I would have begged you to wear *my* shoes."

If *she'd* known she was doing this tonight she would be halfway across the Atlantic!

"Snakeskin, definitely," she murmured.

The other woman nodded and continued her relentless discussion of fashion.

She *would* be crazy to go back to Riccardo. But what choice did she have? The idea that the bank would lend her the money—more than she'd make in ten years of work—was laughable. Even in installments. Her parents were barely getting by on the farm, and although Alex had a great job with one of the city's top PR firms they would never, collectively, be able to scrape up that kind of money.

She had the power to help Lisbeth. Her stomach seemed to go into freefall at the thought of what that might entail. The question was, could she?

Alex gave her an *I need to talk to you* look and politely whisked her away from the designer. "People keep stealing you away," she hissed, dragging Lilly toward the windows. "What *did* he say to you?"

Lilly stared at her sister's flashing blue gaze—the only thing that differentiated them as twins. Her eyes were a mirror image of their sister Lisbeth's. And suddenly her guilt for never having been there for her younger sister made her next move crystal-clear.

She forced herself to smile. Riccardo had made it clear no one was to know about their deal. Not even family. There was too much of a chance for someone to say the wrong thing at the wrong time to the wrong person. The press would blow it wide open.

"We had a really good talk, Alex. I—"

The music stopped. She spun around to find Riccardo standing at the front of the room, his gaze trained on her. She swallowed hard as he nodded for her to join him.

Judgement time.

She steeled herself and raised a trembling hand to push her hair out of her face. "I'll explain afterward," she whispered to her sister. Then she walked to Riccardo's side.

Her presence there said everything.

A satisfied gleam lit her husband's eyes. He raised a hand to quiet the room. The elegantly dressed crowd fell silent as every eye moved to them and hushed anticipation blanketed the air. The first marriage in the history of the De Campo family to disintegrate. A golden couple at that.

She was distracted by a waitress, who presented a bottle for Riccardo's inspection. "The 1972 Chianti."

A 1972 Chianti? The same wine as on their wedding? Her gaze flew to her husband's, which was impaling hers with a burning darkness that seared her soul. He was really doing *this* to her?

What kind of a game was he playing?

The waitress passed each of them a glass of the ruby-red wine. Its deep, rich color was hypnotizing, reminding Lilly of the emotional blood the two of them had spilled. Her hands shook so much around the crystal she was terrified the wine was going to end up down the front of her dress.

Riccardo turned to face their guests, with a controlled, purposeful ease to his movements. "Lilly and I would like to thank you all for coming. You are our closest family, friends and acquaintances and we wanted you to be the first to share in our news."

He paused. The room grew so silent you could have heard a pin drop. Lilly's fingers tightened around the glass, her heart pounding in tandem with her head.

"Sometimes it takes a momentous occasion to bring true feelings to the surface." Riccardo returned his gaze to her face. "For Lilly and I, it took contemplating divorce to realize how much in love we still are."

A gasp rang out. Alex gaped at her from the front row, where she stood with Gabe.

Riccardo cast his gaze over the crowd. "Lilly and I are reconciling."

A shocked buzz filled the room—the sound of a hundred conversations starting at once. Flashbulbs exploded in her face. Hearing the words spoken out loud made her knees go weak. But she kept her gaze trained on her husband's and forced what might have passed for a smile to her lips.

Now her acting role began.

Riccardo tilted his glass toward her. "To new beginnings."

Lilly lifted the glass to her mouth and drank. Her lashes fluttered down over her cheeks as the heady, intoxicating flavor of the Chianti transported her back to the day when her life had seemed poised at the beginning of a rainbow that stretched forever.

The day she had married Riccardo.

And at that moment she knew her mistake for what it was. She had never been, and never would be, in control of her feelings for her husband. Six months wasn't just going to be self-destructive. There was going to be collateral damage.

Riccardo poured himself a two-finger measure of Scotch and sank down in the chair by the window, his gaze on his wife, who lay sleeping in their bed. She had swayed on her feet after the toast, her hands moving to her head in a warning sign that one of those migraines that had always terrified him was about to take her out. He was fairly sure she would have hit the deck had he not slid a subtle arm around her waist and hustled her from the room.

He had left Gabe in charge of winding up the evening and, although Alex had flatly refused to leave her sister, had overridden her and sent her home with his brother. There was still some of Lilly's migraine medication in their medicine cabinet and the key to these attacks, he knew, was to get it into her as soon as possible and put her to bed. Which he'd done—right after she'd been violently ill in their bathroom.

He took a sip of the smoky single malt blend and moved his gaze over her face. It was ghostly white and pinched even in sleep, and for a moment guilt rose up in him. He had dangled the one thing she loved more than anything else in front of her when he knew she wanted nothing to do with him. But then again, he thought, his lips twisting, she hadn't given him any warning when she'd walked out on him. When she'd called it quits on their marriage and left without even having the guts to face him.

A fury long dormant raged to life inside him, pulsing like an untamed beast. Who *did* that? Who took a perfectly good marriage with a few of the usual speed bumps and just quit? Who thought so little of what she had that it was easier to turn into an ice queen and refuse him than to talk it out?

The woman who'd turned into a stranger before his very eyes. The woman who'd taken a lover—a world-renowned cardiothoracic surgeon so highly decorated for his work that he made Riccardo look like the most heartless of corporate raiders. That was who.

His fingers tightened around the glass, drawing his gaze to the fiery amber liquid. No, he wouldn't feel any regret. His wife might have looked at him with those accusing, pain-soaked cat's eyes of hers and begged him to let her go home. But he was through giving her time and space to come to her senses. She was back in his bed, where she belonged, and she was staying there.

Not for six months.

For good.

He lifted the glass to his lips and let the Scotch burn a path down his throat. It had been that conversation he'd overheard that had set him off. Not his father's bullish suggestion that he repair his marriage in order to present the kind of image the De Campo board was looking for in a CEO.

The trash-talking locker room chatter he'd heard on his way out of the gym after a squash game with Gabe had amused him at first. There were things guys said in a locker room that were never repeated outside of them. He had smiled, remembering the crude conversations he and his fellow drivers had had after their races, when all the tension was gone, and then started packing up his stuff. But the conversation had turned to injuries and rehabilitation and he'd heard Lilly's name.

He'd pulled the zipper shut on his bag and had frozen in place as the three men he'd figured must be professional athletes from their height and brawn, went on.

"She's the best there is," one of them had said. "Fixed my bum leg in a month."

"Seriously hot," added one of the others. "I bet you'd like to have more than her hands on you."

He'd been halfway across the room before Gabe had intercepted him and shoved him bodily out the door.

"Not worth it," his brother had muttered. "She's your estranged wife, remember?"

But it had been too much. *Troppo.* It was time Lilly remembered who she was. Who she belonged to.

He skimmed his gaze over her still form. If anything, she had grown more beautiful since that day he'd bumped into her in that SoHo bar. She'd reminded him of a young colt, tripping over those long legs of hers, over *him,* as he'd stopped to put his wallet back in his pocket. She'd apologized, biting her lip in that trademark gesture of hers, and everything about her—her beautiful shoulder-length glossy brown hair, her big hazel eyes and her air of extreme innocence—had knocked him sideways. He wasn't used to women without artifice. And it had made him want to possess her like no other.

He hadn't let her leave the bar until he'd had her reluctantly given number. Then he'd pursued her, called her every day for a week, until she'd agreed to go out with him.

Finding out she was a virgin had been the end for him. He'd put a ring on her finger the week after.

She shifted restlessly onto her back and rubbed her hand against her face. Her vulnerability hit him like a punch to the chest. Lilly was different from any other woman he'd met. She hadn't been attracted to his power or money. In fact it had made her distinctly uncomfortable, given her poor upbringing. But he'd pushed his agenda through anyway, like the big, forceful bull of a man he was. Because that was what a De Campo did. Took what he wanted. Success at all costs.

Lilly fought her way out of the drug-induced fog that held her under, reaching desperately for the glass of water she kept on the nightstand. But her hand grasped only air, and this didn't feel like her bed. It felt bigger, softer, familiar and yet...

It was her old bed.

She bolted upright.

"Here—drink," a husky, fatigue-deepened male voice urged, pressing a glass to her lips.

A strong arm slid around her waist. She blinked and opened her eyes and stared straight into the worried dark-as-night gaze of her husband.

Oh, God. She was in bed with Riccardo.

She pushed the glass away and pulled, panicked, at the sheets.

"Lilly." He placed firm hands on her shoulders and held her down. "Drink for *God's* sake. Those pills are always rough on you."

She shook her head and reached for the side of the bed, but a series of wheezing coughs racked her body. She reached desperately for the glass and drank greedily. Her thirst quenched, she pushed the glass away. "What time is it?"

"One a.m."

A dull, deep throb at the front of her head made her sit back against the pillows. "I want to go home."

"You are home," he said quietly. "Stay in the bed, Lilly. You're in no shape to be going anywhere."

It was then that she realized he was still fully dressed. Hazy memories filled her head. Him holding her hair out of her face while she vomited. Him carrying her to bed. Her cheeks heated with mortification. *She needed to get out of here.*

"My home is my apartment." She swung her legs over the side of the bed, wincing as the movement made her head throb. *Her legs were bare.* And she was drowning in one of Riccardo's white T-shirts. "Did you *undress* me?" she demanded, flicking him an accusing look.

An amused glitter flashed in his eyes. "That's the way it's usually done, *tesoro,* but I stopped at the underwear. I prefer to dispense of that when you're fully conscious."

Her face felt as if it was on fire. She scanned the floor desperately for her things. "Give me my goddamned clothes, Riccardo."

His expression hardened. "Are you forgetting our deal? You live here now. You're mine for six months."

"*Tu sei pazzo,*" she spat at him. "I might have agreed to your crazy plan, but in no way, shape or form will your hands ever be on me again."

"*Tu sei pazzo?*" he murmured appreciatively. "I do believe your Italian's coming along. And, yes, I am crazy when it comes to you." He gently pushed against her shoulders and sent her back into the soft pillows. "Tomorrow we go over the ground rules. Tonight you rest."

"You are such a bully," she muttered wrathfully, too weak to defy him. "I have an early clinic tomorrow."

"I'll drive you there. You still have some clothes in the spare room you can wear."

He'd kept them? She'd left in such a hurry she'd taken only what would fit in a suitcase. Left all the beautiful gowns and jewelry behind.

"Yes, I kept them," he murmured, a bitter smile curving his lips. "Unlike you, I didn't give up on this marriage."

She closed her eyes. "You have no idea what you're talking about, Riccardo."

"Maybe you can enlighten me over the next six months, then. You never did grace me with an explanation."

Her gaze met his with blazing fury. "You never wanted to hear what I had to say."

The belligerent tilt of his chin matched hers. "Maybe now I do."

And maybe there was a blue-cheese moon out there tonight.

A jagged pain whizzed through her head. She winced and held a hand to her temple.

"*Hell*, Lilly," he bit out, waving a hand at her. "We're done arguing. Close your eyes and go to sleep."

She tried to fight it, but nature was having none of it. He tucked the covers up to her chin, then everything went black.

CHAPTER THREE

Seven hours of sleep, one migraine-hangover-filled morning, three patients and one trip to the bank later, Lilly retreated to her office like a maimed fighter who'd escaped to her corner.

Coffee, she decided, setting her briefcase down. It was time to reintroduce the other banned substance in her life. Maybe it would help lift the paralysis that had gripped her since she'd woken up in her old bed this morning, dazed and confused at what had transpired.

She had agreed to become Mrs. Lilly De Campo again. The one thing she'd said she'd never do.

Worse, she'd let her husband see how deep her feelings ran. Distracted, she raised a hand to her hair and pushed it out of her face. The power Riccardo still held over her was disconcerting.

And *that* was the understatement of the year. She pressed her lips together, picked up her purse and let Katy, the receptionist at the small clinic she shared with another physiotherapist in SoHo, know she'd be in the café across the street. Scanning the menu board, she thought, *To hell with it,* and ordered the largest, creamiest latte they had, which would certainly knock her brain back into working order, and sat down to drink it in the window facing Broadway.

It helped. But with her escape hatch rapidly closing it was a case of avoiding the unavoidable. Her only alternative to accepting Riccardo's deal had been to secure the money at the bank. And she was pretty sure the bank manager would have laughed at her request if she hadn't officially reinstated her position as Mrs. Lilly De Campo by having it splashed across the morning papers.

She'd been getting to her feet when he'd given her a curious look and said, "Your husband is also a client, Mrs. De Campo. We'd be happy to draw up the papers with *him*."

She had given him a withering look. "No, thank you, Mr. Brooks. This is a personal matter."

He was an opportunist, she conceded, scraping the froth off the sides of her mug. Like almost everyone else in this city. Unfortunately Harry Taylor had also seen the news, if his multiple calls to her cell phone were any indication. A stomach-churning glance at her phone revealed she now had a message from him too. The latte seemed to curdle inside her. She'd been waiting, hoping there was some other solution that would allow her to call things off with Riccardo.

And who are you trying to fool? a voice inside her ridiculed. Their reconciliation was the subject of intense public speculation this morning. There was no getting out of it. And how could she when it was Lisbeth's only chance at survival?

She squirmed on the stool. What *was* she going to say to Harry? *I'm so sorry, Harry. I've gotten back together with the man who destroyed me?* Or, *I'm sorry for saying I wanted you when really I want my sexy, controlling somewhat ex-husband, who kissed me within an inch of my life last night and made me want more.*

Ugh. There was no good way to put it that wouldn't end up making her look like a horrible, horrible woman.

The café door chimed. She looked up to see the *other* person she was trying to avoid waltzing through the door.

"You really didn't think you could hide, did you?" Alex

asked grimly, tossing an order at the barista and plopping herself down on the stool beside her.

Lilly pushed her empty mug away. "I'm not avoiding you. I had a jam-packed morning."

Alex's eyebrows rose. "I'm your twin, remember? I can sense inner turmoil."

"I'm fine. Just a little groggy from the medication."

"Good." Her sister threw the words at her with a determined tilt of her chin. "So you can tell me what the hell's going on. Your autocratic husband ordered me out of the house before I could see if you'd actually lost your senses."

Lilly pulled in a breath. "It was like Riccardo said. It took a tough conversation for us to realize our feelings for each other."

Alex sat back in her chair and crossed her arms. "*Do not* try to spin me, Lilly. I know you too well. You walked in there last night intent on a divorce. What happened?"

"We talked...we came to some realizations..."

"Like what?" Alex waved her hand in the air. "Like the last hellish year of your marriage was just an apparition? Like he didn't almost annihilate you?"

"It takes two to tango," Lilly murmured. "Riccardo wasn't the only guilty party in our marriage."

"Only the majority holder." Her sister screwed up her face. "What about Harry? Last night you were telling me he's the one."

"I didn't say that. I said I wanted the opportunity to truly pursue things with him." She bit her lip, realizing how confused that sounded. *Dammit, she needed to make this believable. For Lisbeth's sake.*

"You know I've never really stopped loving Riccardo," she said quietly. And the fact that saying it didn't seem like too much of a stretch shook her to her core. "I want to give it another shot."

Alex's mouth tightened. "You left him to save yourself. And I for one don't relish being the one to pick up the pieces again when he reverts to being his domineering, controlling self."

"He's changed," Lilly lied.

"Men like him don't change. They come out of the womb like that."

Her mouth curved. "Probably true."

"What about his infidelity? Are you prepared to put up with that again?"

Everything around her faded, blurred into the series of carefully manufactured images she had created to keep herself in one piece. Control. Because to imagine Riccardo in bed with another woman—to imagine the man who'd promised to love her for life doing that to her—would damage her beyond repair.

"It won't happen again."

"How do you know?"

"Because he promised me."

In actual fact Riccardo had denied the whole thing. He'd put it down to the vicious money-making tactics of the tabloids. But Lilly had seen the photos. And photos didn't lie.

Her teeth clamped down on her bottom lip. The effort it took not to blurt out what was actually going on was immense. "You have to trust me," she forced out huskily. "I'm doing the right thing."

Her sister gave her a long, hard look. "You promise if things start to get bad you'll end it? You'll walk away?"

"I promise. And, Alex—this means we can get Lisbeth's treatment."

A light went on in her sister's cornflower-blue eyes. "Lilly Anderson, you promise me right now you are *not* doing this because of Lisbeth. I do *not* need two sisters in critical condition."

"I wouldn't do that," Lilly said firmly. "It's just a very wonderful outcome of this decision."

But she would. She would do anything it took to make Lisbeth well.

* * *

Riccardo came to pick her up at six. "You still don't look good," he said bluntly as she slid into his beast of a car.

She shrugged and pulled her seatbelt on. "You know what my migraines are like. It takes me a few days to get over one."

He put the car in gear and pulled out into traffic, the low-slung powerful machine reminding her of the man himself. Smooth, dangerous.

He flicked her a glance. "I'd forgotten just how bad they get."

She wondered if he'd done what she had. Used any method available to wipe her head clean of him—finding it impossible on so many levels.

Don't fool yourself, Lil. Riccardo wasn't the type to pine for anyone. Especially the woman who'd walked out on him.

Which begged the question: why hadn't he had other women over the past year? If she was to believe the highly sexed man she'd married was capable of celibacy, the question was why had he chosen it? Riccardo loved women. He lived for the contrast. Hard versus soft. Rational versus emotional. And with his superstar racing background they were like a feast that had been put on this earth for him to enjoy in endless supply.

She had fooled herself that she could be the only one for him.

She twisted her hands together in her lap and stared sightlessly out the window. They drove in a tense silence until he passed her street.

"What about my apartment? I need to get my stuff."

"I sent Mrs. Collins over to pick it up."

Her jaw dropped. He'd had Magda go through her stuff? Sift through the very fiber of her personal life?

"Stop the car."

He frowned over at her. "Lilly, it was—"

"Stop the car."

He swore under his breath and pulled to the curb. "It was the efficient way to get it done."

"Efficient?" she demanded, her voice shaking with anger. "You violated my privacy. My God, how did you even get in to my apartment?"

"I was the one who had the locks installed for you. You're overreacting, Lilly."

She clenched her hands in her lap for fear she might slap his handsome face. He'd pretended to be worried about the dismal state of the locks on her front door and had insisted on having them changed and a deadbolt added. She'd been grateful at the time, because in New York a solid set of locks was never a bad idea. But really it had just been another of his attempts to control her.

"You did that so you could spy on me," she hissed, pressing her head back against the seat. "How could I be so stu—"

"Stop." His eyes blazed into hers. His bronzed skin was pulled taut across his cheekbones. "You know I have security on you. You are still my wife and, like it or not, there are people out there who itch to get their hands on you. But I have never, *ever* spied on you."

"You knew about Harry."

"I *saw* you with Harry. You were eating at Nevaros the same night I was."

"You didn't introduce yourself."

"And say what? *How do you find my wife in bed? What would you rate her out of ten?*"

Her breath caught in her throat. "This is not going to work."

"You agreed to the bargain. You're my wife for the next six months. Deal with it."

She closed her eyes and pressed her palms against her thighs, forcing herself to take deep breaths. If she was to survive the next six months without having to go into emotional rehab she was going to have to learn to control her emotions.

She turned her gaze on him—defiant hazel on arrogant black. "Ground rule number one. You don't *ever* go into my apartment again without my permission and you do *not* enable someone to go through my personal possessions."

He nodded. *"Bene."*

Shocked at how easily he'd acquiesced, she kept going. "I want to go to my apartment now."

"Why?"

"Because I doubt Mrs. Collins packed my book. Or brought my two violets with her. And there's a few things I don't want hanging around."

"Like the sex toys you use with Harry?" he taunted.

"Why, yes. Harry knows how to keep things interesting."

He froze.

Her fingers curled around the door handle.

In a lightning-fast movement his hand slammed down on top of hers. "You know what a comment like that does to a guy like me, Lilly. Are you looking for me to up the ante? Because I can assure you Taylor doesn't make you scream like I do."

Lilly slunk back in her seat, her heart hammering in her chest.

He lifted his hand away from hers and returned it to the wheel. "Choose your fights carefully, *tesoro.* You know how many times you've won."

Never. She never won against Riccardo because he was too strong, too smart, and he knew her too well ever to let it happen.

They didn't speak during their brief stopover at her apartment, nor on the drive to the house.

Magda enveloped her in a warm hug when they walked through the door and told them dinner was ready when they were. Lilly went upstairs to change.

Riccardo was waiting for her in the small, private dining room when she came down. Magda had closed the doors to the terrace as the chill of the early May evening set in, and lit candles on the table in the warm dark-floored room with its elegant white wainscoting and glowing sconces. For a moment she stood standing in the entranceway, a sharp little pain tugging at her insides. She had been so desperate for her husband's attention in the latter days of their marriage that all she had dreamed about was coming home to a meal like this with him.

She took him in as he opened a bottle of wine, his muscular forearms flexing in the candlelight as he worked the cork out of the bottle. He hadn't bothered to change, but had taken off his suit jacket and tie and rolled his shirtsleeves up. In charcoal-gray trousers and white shirt he looked better than any man had a right to look. They molded his leanly muscular body into a work of art. She sank her teeth into her bottom lip. Women actually stopped in the street to stare at her husband. He was just *that* good-looking. In the beginning she hadn't minded, because she'd known she had him and they didn't.

In the end it had been crucifying.

Her gaze slid up to his face. He was watching her, the bottle in his hands, his dark eyes seeming to reach inside of her and read her every emotion. She shifted her weight to the other foot and stood her ground. Six-foot-four and broad-shouldered, he made the room seem stiflingly small.

He'd always been vastly intimidating. Except when he'd been naked beneath her. Those times *she* had been in control—her thighs straddling all that golden muscular flesh, his taut, powerful body beneath her tense, begging her for the release that had always bordered on the spiritual with them.

A glint entered his dark eyes. Her lashes swept down over hers. *What in God's name was she doing?*

"Rule number two, *cara*," he murmured. "No looking at me like that unless you intend to follow through with it."

Wildfire raced to her cheeks. *Dammit.* She walked jerkily across to him and took the glass of wine he'd poured.

Magda came in with their salads, her round face beaming. "How nice to see the two of you sitting down to a meal together."

"Yes, what a novelty," Lilly agreed. "I hardly remember how to converse."

Magda gave her a wary look, told them the casserole was in the oven and left.

"You will curb your tongue when others are around," Riccardo said curtly when the housekeeper was safely out of earshot. "Our deal depends on us being discreet."

"You liked it in the bedroom," she taunted.

"Right on the money, *tesoro*," he agreed, showing his teeth. "Knock yourself out."

She shrugged. "Since we won't be sharing a bedroom, I'll pass."

He took a sip of his wine, then lowered the glass with a slow, deliberate movement. "Here I am, speaking *your* native language, and still you don't get it."

"Get what?"

"We need to make this authentic, Lilly. We *will* be sharing a bedroom."

Her stomach dissolved into a ball of nerves. There was absolutely no way, with all the rooms in this house, that she was sharing *that* bedroom with *him*.

"Magda is completely trustworthy. There is no need to—"

"This isn't up for debate." He leaned back against the sideboard and crossed his arms over his chest. "Eyes are everywhere. People traipse through this house on a daily basis."

Lilly gave him a desperate look. "But I—"

"Rule number three." He kept going like a train, steamrollering right over her. "You will accompany me to all the social engagements I'm committed to over the next six months, and if I need to travel you'll do that too."

"I have patients who count on me, Riccardo. I can't just pick up and travel at will."

He shrugged. "Then you work around it. Our first engagement, by the way, is Saturday. It's a charitable thing for breast cancer."

She bit back the primal urge to scream that was surging against the back of her throat. She had a career, for God's sake. Responsibilities. And no wardrobe for a charity event. She was at least ten pounds heavier than she'd been when she'd been with Riccardo. None of her gowns upstairs would fit, and nothing she'd been wearing in her low-key life since then would be appropriate.

"Oh," he added, almost as an afterthought. "It's a fashion thing. They called today to ask if you'd model a gown when they heard our news."

She felt the blood drain from her face. "On a stage?"

"That's usually how they would do it, isn't it?"

The thought of modeling a gown in front of all those people with her new, curvier figure sent a sharp response tumbling out of her. "No."

He frowned. "What do you mean, no? It's for a good cause."

"Then *you* get up there and do it."

His gaze darkened. "Are you going to fight me on everything?"

"When you ask me to get up on a stage and parade myself around in front of a bunch of people when you know I hate that stuff, *yes*."

He tipped his head to one side. "You're a beautiful woman, Lilly. I never understood why you were so insecure."

And he never would. He had no clue how deep her insecurities ran. The demons she'd finally put to rest. And that was the way she preferred to keep it. Weakness left you vulnerable. Exposed. Open for people to pick at and slowly destroy you.

"I won't do it."

"You will," he returned grimly. "Ground rule number four. You will have no further contact with Harry Taylor."

The man she still hadn't had the guts to call back yet. "I have to talk to him. He's been trying to call me and he sounds—"

"Trying?" He lifted a brow. "I see your old patterns of avoidance haven't changed."

"Go to hell," she muttered. "You sandbagged me with this last night. I need a chance to explain it to him."

"One conversation, Lilly. And if I find out you've seen him after that—if I find out you've even chatted with him in the hallway—our agreement will be null and void."

It was fine for *him* to cheat in the public eye but when it came to her the same rules didn't apply!

He flicked a hand at her. "It's not like it should be a tough call, ending things. Or have you become such a tease you can kiss a man like you did me last night and still go back for more?"

She shook her head. "You're such a bastard sometimes."

A savage smile curled his lips. "You like it when I'm a son-of-a-bitch, *amore mio.* It excites you."

She turned her back on him before she said something she'd regret. She'd loved that about him in the beginning. That he'd called the shots and all she'd had to do was sit back and enjoy the ride. For a girl who'd been taking care of herself most of her life it had been a relief. An escape from the hand-to-mouth existence that had seen her work two jobs to put herself through college and graduate school to supplement the scholarship she'd won.

What she hadn't been prepared for was the flashy, no-end-to-the-riches lifestyle he'd dropped her into with no preparation, no defences for a girl from Iowa who'd never really grown into the hard-edged, sink-or-swim Manhattan way of life.

It had been her downfall. Her inability to cope.

"Ground rule number five," he continued softly. "You and I are going to be the old Riccardo and Lilly. The perfect couple. We're going to act madly in love, there will be no other men, and when you get weak and can't stand it anymore you'll come to me." He paused and flashed a superior smile. "I give you a week, max."

She spun around to face him, her gaze clashing with his. "I'm not the same person I was, Riccardo. You won't find me groveling at your feet for attention. And you won't walk all over me like you did before. You treat me as an equal or I'll leave and blow this deal to smithereens."

He lifted his elegant shoulders, as if he found her little outburst amusing. "But you want this house. Badly... I saw it in your eyes last night."

For a reason entirely other than what you think.

"Are you finished?" she asked quietly. "Because I suddenly seem to have lost my appetite. I'm going to go make sense of my stuff upstairs."

His gaze narrowed on her face. "Don't make yourself into a martyr. I've had enough of that to last a lifetime."

She lifted her chin. "Martyrs die for their cause. When this is over I'll be free of you. Eternally happy is more like it."

Lilly took her time unpacking her things, her arms curiously heavy as she hung her delicate pieces on hangers in the huge walk-in closet. Every item she unpacked was an effort, and her stomach was growing tighter with each piece she added with her usual military precision. Sweaters with sweaters, blouses with blouses, pants with pants. It was as if her old life was reappearing in front of her hanger by hanger, row by row.

And there was nothing she could do to stop it.

She'd said she'd never come back. What the hell was she doing?

She plunged on, doggedly working until everything was in its place. Then, when she was sure Riccardo was working in his study—which he undoubtedly would be until midnight—she slipped downstairs and made herself a snack. She wasn't remotely hungry, but skipping meals was a warning signal for her. She put some cheese and crackers on a plate, poured herself a glass of wine and took it to bed.

She had finished her snack and read about half a chapter of her supposedly scintillating book when her husband walked through the door. *It was only just past eleven. What was he doing?*

"You're coming to bed?"

A mocking smile twisted his mouth. "That's what it looks like, no?"

She shifted uncomfortably. "You usually work later than this."

"Maybe having my beautiful bride back in my bed is a draw."

Heat flared in her cheeks at the sarcasm in his voice. "As if," she muttered under her breath.

"What?"

"Nothing."

He flicked her a glance. "Mumbling is rude, Lilly. If you have something to say, say it."

She stuck her nose in her book. She didn't have to play this game. Except it was impossible not to sneak a glance at his bronzed, muscled chest as he whipped his shirt off. In keeping with his new harsher haircut, his body seemed even harder than before. As if someone had taken a chisel and worked away the remaining minute amounts of excess flesh until all that was left was smooth, hard, defined muscle, tapering down to that six pack she loved.

Hell. She buried her face back in her book. The rasp of his zipper and the sound of his pants hitting the floor had her desperately reading the same sentence over and over. His boxers flew across the room and landed in the hamper. Her breath seized in her throat. *She would not—would not—look.*

She took a deep breath as he sauntered into the bathroom and shut the door. Her passing out moment last night had meant she hadn't seen any of *that.* Her hectic pulse indicated she hadn't gotten any more immune to the show in the past twelve months.

This was just *so* not good it was laughable. No wonder she hadn't come near him in months. Because *this* happened.

She'd made it through a miraculous two pages when her husband emerged from the bathroom, the smell of his spicy aftershave filling her nostrils. A flash of skin in her peripheral vision revealed he hadn't lost his predisposition for sleeping in the nude.

She took another of those steadying breaths as he walked around the bed to his side, but all that did was overwhelm her with the cologne some manufacturer had for sure pumped full of every pheromone in the book. The bed dipped as the owner of the pheromones whipped the sheets back and got in. She made a grab for the material, feeling far too exposed in her short silk nightie, but not before her husband swept his eyes over her in a mocking perusal. She gritted her teeth and pulled the sheets up high over her chest.

Her husband's rich, deep laughter made her grit her teeth even harder. "I saw it all last night, Lil, and I have to say I like the changes. You look like a properly voluptuous Italian woman now. Your breasts are fabulous—and those hips…" He sat back against the headboard, a wicked smile pulling at the corner of his lips. "Without a doubt my favorite spot on a woman's body. That curve near the hipbone you can slide your hand over, and—"

"Stop." She flashed him a murderous look. "I may be

living with you for six months but these—these types of conversations are *not* happening."

He lifted his shoulders and pursed his lips. "This is the point where you'd usually freeze me out anyway."

She flinched. "It was always about sex. Sometimes I actually wanted to communicate."

"That's where men and women differ," he drawled. "When we're stressed we crave sex. It's the way *we* communicate."

"It was the *only* way you communicated. Too bad it wasn't conducive to working out our problems."

His face hardened. "You didn't want to work them out. You checked out, Lilly. You wanted us to fail."

"I wanted us to *work*." She blinked back the emotion stinging her eyes. "But we were light years apart. And we always have been. We were just too stupid to realize it."

He reached over and grabbed the book, tossing it on his bedside table. "You haven't read a thing since I walked into this room, *cara*. You're so busy trying to deny what's between us that you can't see a foot in front of you. That isn't light years apart—that's total avoidance."

"The easier way," she flashed. "Because we both know how it ends."

She took satisfaction in the frustrated flash of his eyes before she turned away from him and doused the light, curling up as far away from him as she could in the big king-sized bed. It was still impossible to ignore his presence. His warmth, his still, even breathing was everywhere around her.

She curled her fingers into the sheets and focused on keeping it together, shocked by the need, the almost physical ache for him to reach out and comfort her in the way he always had. When Riccardo had made love to her she had always known where his heart was. The problem had been when the cold light of day had dawned and their problems hadn't gone away.

She squeezed her eyes shut. Tomorrow she had to tell Harry it was over between them. It should have been a horrible thing to have to do. But with Riccardo back in her life, bearing down on her like a massive all-consuming storm, she knew her relationship with Harry was doomed.

There had only ever been one man who'd had her heart. Too bad he hadn't been worthy of it.

CHAPTER FOUR

RICCARDO WOKE UP Saturday morning with the need to hit something. To flatten something. Anything that got rid of the tension sitting low in his belly after he'd been jarred awake by some fool's motorcycle racing down the street.

Eternally happy. His wife's words echoed through his head, made worse by the paper-white state of her face when she'd returned home last night after ending things with Taylor.

He wanted to put a fist through the doctor's face.

He rolled over to glare at her, but there was only an imprint in the pillow where her head had been. Lilly? Out of bed before him? She liked to sleep more than any human being he knew.

He flicked a glance at the clock on the bedside table, his eyes widening as he read the neon green numbers. *Eight-thirty.* That couldn't be right. Sure, he was tired, because his wife was driving him crazy, but eight-thirty? A glance at his watch confirmed it was true.

Swinging his legs over the side of the bed, he struggled to clear the foreign-feeling fuzz in his head. He'd plowed through a mountain of work last night before coming to bed. To avoid the urge to come up here and make his wife eat her words. To pleasure her until she screamed and forgot Harry Taylor even existed.

A chainsaw would do it.

He picked up his mobile and called Gabe. There was a half-dead oak on their Westchester property that was a serious safety hazard. He'd been meaning to ask the landscapers to take it down, but suddenly the thought of a physical, mind-blanking task appealed to him greatly.

"Matteo got in last night," Gabe said. "I'll bring him and we can have some beer afterward."

"As long as you don't let him anywhere near the saw."

His youngest brother, who ran De Campo's European operations, and their father were in town for the annual board meetings. Which was probably another reason his gut was out of order. Whatever his father said in those meetings would make or break his chances of becoming CEO. And it had better go in his favor.

"We'll make him the look-out," Gabe said drily. "See you in forty-five."

Riccardo showered, put on an old pair of jeans and a T-shirt, and went to procure a travel cup of coffee in the kitchen. Lilly wasn't in there, or in the library she loved.

He was wondering if she'd made another run for it when she rushed into the front entryway just as his brothers arrived, a black look on her face, a curse on her breath.

"Matteo!" she exclaimed, her frown disappearing as his youngest brother stepped forward and scooped her up into a hug. "I had no idea you were in town."

Matteo gave her a squeeze and set her down. "If that means you two are busy making up for lost time, I'm good with that."

A flare of color speared Lilly's cheeks. She and Riccardo's youngest brother were close—or had been until their separation. Matteo was the more philosophical and expressive of the three brothers. Women naturally gravitated to him. Used his shoulder to cry on far too much, in Riccardo's opinion.

"It's so good you're here," Lilly said, pulling back and flashing his brother a warm smile. She gave Riccardo's boots and jeans a brief glance, her gaze staying well away from his glowering face, then looked back at Matteo. "Maybe I'll see you when you're back?"

Riccardo's shoulders shot to his ears. Where did she get off, giving his brother a smile like that when she hadn't offered him one in days?

He glanced at her purse and sunglasses. "You're going out?"

"I need to buy a dress for tonight."

"You have hundreds upstairs."

Her mouth tightened. "They don't fit."

He couldn't understand how at least *one* of those dresses didn't fit. Yes, she'd put on a few pounds since they'd been together, but they were undoubtedly in all the right places. *Women.* He lifted his shoulders. "You do still have the credit card?"

She flashed him a sweetly apologetic look. "Cut it into a million little pieces... But I have my own."

The urge to put her over his knee glowed like a red neon sign in front of him. Gritting his teeth, he dug in his pocket and fished the keys to his Jag out. He handed them to her. "Take the car. We'll go in Gabe's."

Her fingers curled around the keys, a hesitant look crossing her face. She loved driving that car. He knew it as surely as he knew where to kiss her to make her crazy. At the base of that beautiful long neck of hers, and most definitely between—

"Okay, thanks." She gave Gabe a kiss on the cheek and left, the car keys jangling from her fingers. Fury swept through him, raging through his veins. She might not think she had to put on a show for his brothers, but by God she was going to start acting the part—or she had a serious lesson coming her way.

Gabe gave him an amused look. "Glad to see you have everything under control."

"I can't believe you gave her the Jag," Matteo added,

leading the way outside. "She looked like she might drive it into a wall just for the fun of it."

Riccardo muttered something under his breath and took the front seat of the Maserati beside Gabe.

"She looks fantastic, though," Matteo said, sliding into the back. "Being away from you agrees with her."

"We all know you're in love with my wife," Riccardo shot back. "Why don't you spend your time finding one for yourself rather than drooling over mine?"

"Lilly needs someone in her corner with you as a *coniuge*," his brother returned, unperturbed. "You haven't exactly been husband of the year material."

Riccardo turned in his seat as Gabe backed out of the driveway. "What, exactly, does *that* mean?"

"You work fourteen-, sixteen-hour days and you treat Lilly as an afterthought," Matteo said belligerently. "I can't believe she put up with two years of it."

Riccardo was halfway into the backseat when Gabe threw up his hand. "*Sit the hell down. I'm* going to drive into a wall if you keep this up."

Riccardo sat back, pulling in a deep breath. "Keep your mouth shut until you know all the facts."

"You never talk so how would I know them?"

"Try living with the Ice Queen."

"She wasn't always like that," Matty murmured. "Maybe you should ask yourself what happened."

"Maybe you should mind your own business."

That set the tone for the forty-five-minute drive north of the city to Westchester. Riccardo kept his gaze on the scenery while Gabe and Matty caught up. Suburban New York blurred into a continuous stream of exclusive green bedroom communities. But if the scenery was tranquil, his mood was not.

What did they think? He was going to make the De Campo name a player in the North American restaurant business by being home for dinner at six every night?

That he was going to claim his birthright by being any less driven and focused than his father Antonio? He rubbed his hand across his unshaven jaw and shook his head.

"You never wanted to hear what I had to say," Lilly had lashed out at him the other night. "I'm through groveling at your feet, begging for your attention…"

Dio. Was he really that bad?

There'd been a time when he'd been much more laid-back. When he'd been driving a racecar for one of Italy's top teams and all he'd been focused on was winning. The shockingly alive feeling of driving a car at one-hundred-eighty miles an hour finally free of his father's iron grip. He had eaten up life with the appetite of a man determined to savor every minute.

And every beautiful woman who came along with it— like the froth on top of his espresso.

But Lilly had not been one of those easy-to-attain women who had chased him from track to track. Lilly had been the ultimate challenge. The one woman he could never have enough of. Her sharp wit, her loving nature— before she'd turned cold—and her bewitching sensuality had made her the hottest woman he'd ever touched. He had been consumed with the need to possess her, body and soul. And it had almost made him make the biggest mistake of his life.

He shifted in his seat. The sheer stupidity of what he'd almost done was something that would haunt him forever. He had kissed Chelsea Tate with the intent of taking her to bed at the absolute lowest point of his marriage. When Lilly wouldn't talk to him and he'd felt so alienated in his own home he hadn't been thinking straight. He'd wanted to prove he didn't need her, that he didn't love her so much that it was sending him straight to hell. But all it had done was backfire on him when he'd kissed Chelsea and realized Lilly was the only woman for him.

A bitter taste that had nothing to do with the espresso he

was consuming filled his mouth. Lilly, on the other hand, seemed to have moved on as easily as if she was shifting to the next course at dinner.

His fingers dug into the flimsy paper cup. If he had to sleep in that bed with her one more night with her freezing him out—warning him away from those sweet, soft curves that were his and his alone—he wasn't going to be responsible for his actions.

The tension in the car spilled out into the brisk morning as they parked in front of the Westchester house and stepped from the car. Riccardo took a big breath of the clean, woodsy air and felt the tension seep away as the soul-restoring properties of his home on the lake kicked in. He'd fallen in love with the beautiful rolling countryside on his first visit here, to a business associate's home on the Hudson River. When this estate had come up for sale he'd snapped it up as an escape for him and Lilly. But he'd been so busy they'd rarely ever made it out here.

Another promise to her he hadn't kept.

To hell with Matty.

Locating the chainsaw, he applied his frustration to the tree and they managed to take the huge old American white oak down without hitting the house—which was a good thing, since it had to be ninety feet tall and at least three feet in diameter.

Afterward they sat beside the huge old tree, now sprawled in front of them, drinking cold beer out of the can. As different as they all were—Gabe, the intense, serious one, obsessed with the craft of winemaking, who'd known what he'd wanted to do from the time he'd been a little boy; Riccardo, the rebel oldest son; Matty, the in-touch-with-his-feminine side youngest—they were as close as three brothers could be. Even scattered around the globe, with Gabe spending most of his time in Napa Valley, where their vineyards were located and Matty in Tuscany, where he oversaw the company's European operations.

Maybe it was because their mother Francesca, who had come from one of Europe's oldest families, hadn't been the nurturing type. Maybe that was what had bonded the three of them so tightly. Because they were all each other had alongside Antonio's domination. It was sink or swim in the De Campo family, and they had learned to survive—together.

Gabe set down his beer and looked at Riccardo. "Any idea where Antonio's head's at?"

He shook his head. They called their father Antonio because he was not only their father, he was the dominant, larger-than-life figure who had transformed the small, moderately successful De Campo vineyard his grandfather had passed along to him into a force to be reckoned with in the global wine industry.

Gabe shrugged. "Everybody knows it's going to be you. You've been the *de facto* head of the company since Antonio started scaling back."

Riccardo searched his brother's face for any sign that the logical heir to the De Campo empire harbored any bitterness toward him after his father's decision to put Riccardo in control of the company when he'd fallen ill—despite the fact that Gabe had been the obvious choice with Riccardo off racing. But his brother's face was matter-of-fact. As if he'd long ago given up fighting his father's predisposition for his eldest son.

Riccardo took a long swig of his beer. "It's impossible to predict what Antonio will do."

Particularly when teaching his eldest son a lesson seemed to be a greater priority than doing what was right. Antonio had never forgiven Riccardo for wasting his Harvard education on a racing career. No matter how good a driver he'd been—he'd been on track to win his first championship title when his father had fallen ill—Antonio had never forgiven him for his decision. He'd seen racing as a frivolous, ego-boosting activity that pandered to his son's

ego and was disrespectful to the family—to everything
Antonio had raised him to be. He hadn't talked to his eldest son for years, and had only relented when Riccardo
had returned to take the reins of De Campo.

Now Antonio was letting Riccardo sweat his guts out
in purgatory.

Rolling to his feet, he reached for the chainsaw. "Let's
get this done."

He worked his way from one end of the tree to the other,
with his brothers hauling and stacking the pieces. His muscles relaxed and his head cleared. He was nothing if not
a man who knew how to solve a problem. His wife might
think this was the way it was going to be, but she had it
all wrong. This icy détente was ending. And it was ending tonight.

Lilly adjusted the plunging bodice of the lavender gown
for the millionth time and asked herself why in the world
she'd allowed the owner of Sam's to convince her this gown
was *it*.

She felt conspicuous and exposed. Okay, sexy and de-
sirable too. But maybe it was *too much*. And the last thing
she wanted to do was attract any more attention than she
and Riccardo already would tonight. Their first appearance
as a reunited couple since their divorce party was going to
cause enough waves.

And as for when she came to model Antonia Abelli's
gown… All eyes would be on her, searching for and ex-
posing her flaws. And they were going to have a field-day
with her. With her less than perfect body, she could only
imagine what they'd say.

Her stomach rose to her throat. Her fitting with the designer had been humiliating. The eclectic woman, whose
romantic designs she'd always loved, had circled around
her, frowning at the tight fit of the chosen dress. "We'll

have to let some seams out," she'd muttered. "But it'll work."

Lilly had left, cheeks burning, wanting to tell her to make someone else wear the dress—someone it fit! The only problem with that was this was the *new* Lilly. The Lilly who wasn't going to care. The Lilly who was going to go out with Riccardo tonight, act like the perfect wife and not let anyone see how it got to her. She was older and wiser now—she'd gained perspective in the past year. She could handle this. And Lisbeth was all that mattered.

She heard Riccardo turn the water off in the shower. "Shoes," she murmured, ignoring the anticipatory surge of her pulse. And then she'd be ready.

She searched through a shelf full of shoes: slingbacks and stilettos in every shade of the rainbow. Her husband had walked in after his day with his brothers, taken one wary look at the pile of couture creations stacked on the floor for Magda to give away, and had said only, "Ready to leave in fifteen?"

"Aha!" She located her silver slingbacks on the top shelf. At least her shoes fit. They were her absolute weakness and, oh, did she love the strappy soft leather of these, which molded to her feet and felt like heaven...

She sat down on the bed and pulled them on. They made her legs seem a mile long, and if there was anything she needed tonight it was that. The fact she couldn't walk in them was of little consequence. Anything that increased her confidence level was worth it.

Her fingers clumsily refused to obey her as she struggled to thread the thin strap through the tiny loop. The fashion show was one thing. How she and Riccardo were going to fool all those people they knew and make them think they were still in love when they were in the middle of the War of the Roses was another matter entirely.

She managed to get one shoe done up, then started on the other, enduring the same frustrating process. Maybe

what she needed were glasses, because the strap didn't
seem to want to—

"Dammit."

"Need help?"

Riccardo's rich, sexy drawl sent the strap pinging out of
her hand completely. "No, thanks," she murmured, snatch-
ing it up again and yanking it desperately through the loop.
This time the pin slid right into the hole and stayed. Thank
goodness. She didn't need a naked Riccardo any closer than
he was right now because—

Hell. The blood had rushed to her head, bent over like
that, but now, sitting up, her gaze moved over her husband
leaning against the doorway of the bathroom and it seemed
to congeal right there, pounding in her ears. *Not naked.*
He'd wrapped a towel around his waist, but that was almost
worse, because far, far too much mouthwatering muscled,
bronzed flesh was still on display. Everything she hadn't
let herself look at the other night.

She gulped in a desperate breath as that six-pack she'd
loved to tell him turned her on stared her in the face. Her
gaze moved lower, over the grooves in his abdomen only
the most defined men had, skipped the next part, because
really she couldn't go there, and ended up at his gorgeous
thighs and calves. Riccardo had the best legs of any man
she'd ever encountered. Muscled, strong and perfectly
shaped. *Heavenly.*

*No looking at me like that unless you intend to follow
through with it.*

She stood abruptly, teetering on the high shoes. "We
should go. We're late already, and if we're going to get
through traffic—" *He was so not listening to her.* His long-
lashed dark gaze was conducting a thorough inspection
of her physical assets that had begun with her face, swept
down over the plunging neckline of her dress, over the flare
of her hips in the clinging gown to her lavender-tipped feet.

Heat rushed to her face as his gaze lingered. Riccardo had always had a thing for feet.

Her feet in particular.

He turned, walked to the dresser and pulled something out of a drawer. Her heart-rate increased as he walked back toward her, a purposeful look on his face.

"We need to go," she repeated in a strangled voice. "We're already late."

He stopped in front of her, took her by the shoulders and turned her around.

"You need a necklace," he murmured, lifting her hair aside. "What are you worried about, Lilly? That I might tear this dress off you and end this détente?"

It wasn't as if he hadn't done it before… She shivered as he slid the necklace around her throat, the cold stones resting against her heated skin. "Riccardo…"

"Riccardo what?" Humor deepened his voice. "Tear the dress off?"

"Get the hell away from me."

"Because you don't trust yourself when I touch you?"

"Because this is a *charade*," she hissed. "And when we aren't in public you *don't* touch me."

He fastened the clasp of the necklace. "Do you remember how we christened this?"

She stared down at the row of diamonds encircling her throat, sparkling against her skin like a ring of fire. As if she could ever forget. They had been out for dinner, wholly unable to keep their hands off each other, and he'd slapped his credit card on the table as soon as the entrées were removed and taken her home, where he'd ravished her with such urgent, sensual demand she had never been able to wear the necklace again without going back to that moment.

The fleeting sensation of his lips on her bare shoulder made her jump under his hands.

"You look stunningly beautiful in this dress, *tesoro*.

You could easily convince me to forget all about tonight and play hookey."

She would have replied, except his teeth nipped gently into her skin and a wave of heat swept through her. That would be one way of avoiding the fashion show...

Not worth the consequences.

She yanked herself out of his arms and fixed him with a glare. *Remember how he broke your heart. Remember this is only for six months...*

He watched her with a hooded gaze. "I take it that's a no?"

"Not ever," she agreed icily. "Shall we go?"

He inclined his head, stepped toward the closet and stripped off the towel. She averted her eyes and left to wait for him downstairs—but not before she got a full-on shot of his firm, beautiful behind.

CHAPTER FIVE

THE BALLROOM OF the historic hotel near Central Park glittered with light, muted laughter and a sense that time hadn't really moved on—it was just different souls passing through it.

Lilly stood at the entrance with Riccardo and took in the ambience with that same feeling. Massive chandeliers five feet in width still dominated the room, still exuded the elegance of decades past, the band was timelessly tasteful, filling the space with rich classical music, and the black-coated wait staff could have been from any time period. It was *her* that was different. Once she had walked in here with naive, trusting eyes that had seen only the sparkling beauty of so much loveliness in one place. Now she saw it for what it was—a backdrop for the rich and powerful, a symbol of how beauty could destroy and disfigure.

If you let it.

Her gaze shifted to the long runway that ran the center of the room. In an hour she would be up there, modeling Antonia Abelli's dress. If she didn't throw up first. It was a distinct possibility.

Heads turned. The open stares began. Her fingers dug into Riccardo's forearm as the room seemed to ignite with speculative conversation. The press had been all over them since the divorce party, coming up with a multitude of creative, vicious angles as to why they were back together.

Lilly was pregnant—thus her "added pounds," one tabloid had said. Riccardo had had his fill of his mistress and wanted to start a family, said another. Worst of all had been the dirt they'd dug up on poor Harry Taylor—a former girlfriend citing his low libido as the reason Lilly had left him.

Riccardo looked down at her. "Just ignore them," he said quietly. "Ignore the rubbish they say and be true to yourself."

Lilly wished she had just an ounce of his self-confidence right now—or his supreme ability to focus on what was important and let everything else go.

"Let's get a drink," he murmured, sliding an arm around her waist. She leaned into him and allowed herself to absorb the innate strength that had once made her think nothing and no one could ever hurt her.

How wrong she'd been.

They procured martinis at the bar and were soon caught up in a rolling series of conversations with people eager to see if the rumors were true. Were the De Campos *really* back together?

Lilly tried to focus on the conversation, but the closer it got to nine o'clock and the fashion show the weaker her legs felt. She could feel the cold, assessing looks being thrown her way by the socialites who had claimed the limelight in her absence. And her stomach started to churn.

Riccardo shot her a look with those perceptive eyes of his, warning her to liven up. But Lilly was finished with the acting job she'd done for years. He wanted her as a wife? Then he was getting the real Lilly—not some plastic, manufactured replica of herself.

"Riccardo!"

The shrill voice of an outrageously beautiful blond just about took her ears off. About her own age, and so delicate a puff of wind might blow her away in her silver lamé dress, she threw herself into Riccardo's arms and landed a big kiss on either cheek before Lilly could blink.

Riccardo set the diminutive blond down, a smile pulling at the corners of his mouth. "Always a dramatic greeting, Victoria."

A rough-hewn, handsome man in a tux stepped up to shake his hand and clap him on the back. "She always did prefer you, De Campo."

Riccardo smiled—a guarded smile that didn't quite reach his eyes. "Alessandro Marino. This is the last place I'd expect to see you."

"My wife." Alessandro inclined his head with a rueful look. "We had a family wedding in the city. And of course my fashion-obsessed wife couldn't miss this."

Riccardo pulled Lilly forward, his hand firm at her back. "I don't believe you've met *my* wife. Lilly, this is Alessandro Marino, my former teammate, and his wife Victoria."

Lilly felt his fingers digging into her back. Surprised, she looked up at his face. He looked firmly in control, as always, but there was a tightness in his face that belied his easy smile. *Alessandro Marino.* It hit her. The man who had taken Riccardo's place as the star of TeamXT. She'd seen a cover story on him recently. He'd been described as "unbeatable."

Alessandro leaned forward and pressed a kiss to both her cheeks. His wife followed suit.

"So *you're* the woman stupid enough to walk out on Riccardo…" Victoria stood back, giving Lilly a once-over, her blue eyes assessing her as thoroughly as she might a prize filly. "Another few months and you might have been out of luck, with all those women lining up to catch him when he fell."

"Victoria." Alessandro bit out the word. "Not appropriate."

His wife shrugged. "It's the truth."

"How is the wine business?" Alessandro asked Riccardo. "De Campo's doing well."

"We had a good year. And you," he said, nodding at the other man. "You're at the top of the pack. Congratulations."

Alessandro shrugged. "You left big shoes to fill. No one is a daredevil like you, De Campo. I had to work on my style."

"Well, it's obviously working."

"He was the best, you know." Alessandro flicked a glance at Lilly. "He'd have a couple championship titles by now if he'd stayed."

Lilly nodded. "So I've heard."

Racing had always been a taboo subject with her and Riccardo. Anytime she'd brought it up her husband had shut down. As he looked like he was about to do right now, judging by the granite-hard expression on his face.

Their conversation with the Marinos deteriorated into an awkward, stilted back and forth that Lilly escaped as soon as she could with a trip to the ladies' room. When she returned to her husband's side he excused himself from the group of men he was speaking to and took her arm.

"Finished your little temper tantrum?"

"It wasn't a temper tantrum. I'm bored, and I'm tired about hearing how much women love you. I get it."

"Then why is smoke coming out of your ears?" He exerted pressure on her arm until she followed him through the crowd.

"Why didn't you defend me?" she burst out. "Why didn't you say something, like, *Good thing I'm madly in love with my wife,* or *anything* that would have made me feel less like an idiot?"

"What do you care? This is just an act for you, isn't it?"

She glared up at him. "I *don't* care. What bugs me is that all these people think we're back together and madly in love and *you're* letting *her* get away with *that*. You always do with women who fall all over you. You *eat* it up, Riccardo. You get that same look on your face like you had when you were standing on the podium splashing champagne over everyone after winning a race."

His jaw tightened. "All men like attention, Lilly. Especially when you get none from your wife."

Oh. She swung away from him before she hit him. "Is it unrealistic to expect you to stand up for me? You never reassure me. It's humiliating."

He led her onto the dance floor. "You know what's humiliating? Me having to tell everyone we know you've left and not knowing what to say because I didn't know why."

She absorbed that as he pulled her into his arms and wrapped his fingers around hers. "You brought it on yourself, Riccardo. Don't try and make me feel bad for you. One week with me out of the house and you were probably acting like 'Ravishing Riccardo' again."

His gaze sharpened at her use of the tabloid nickname for him. "You have a wicked mouth—you know that, *cara?*"

She stared mutinously at his chest as he pulled her closer. So he'd had to answer some questions about why she'd left? It couldn't possibly have matched the jealousy and humiliation *she'd* felt every time he'd left the house without her, wondering if he was with Chelsea. Wondering why she wasn't enough for him.

She studied his hard, proud profile. Maybe it hadn't been right for her to run as she had. She was sure it had been a knock to his pride for a man who was built around pride and honor, who had a public image to uphold, to admit his marriage had failed. But if she'd stayed in that house one more day she would have cracked in half.

Guilt lanced through her. "What did you tell them, then, when they asked where I was?"

He looked down at her, his expression cold and forbidding. "I told them we were taking some time off. And I let them talk. It was our business, not theirs."

"And you think I should do the same?"

"Let them think what they want. They can't hurt you if you don't let them."

"Have you ever read what they say about me?" she challenged. "Even once?"

"I don't have time to read those rags."

Her mouth tightened. "Today they called my figure 'less than fashionable' and insinuated I was pregnant."

"So what?"

So what? She clamped her mouth shut before she said something she'd regret.

"You need to recognize jealousy for what it is," he said impatiently. "They want to be you. That's why they try and tear you down."

She gave him a vicious look. "What would you know about it? You're Mr. Perfect. You have an affair and it only makes you sexier to them."

His eyes went so black she took a step backward. His fingers tightened around hers, drawing her forward in a slow, deliberate movement that wouldn't attract attention. His tone as he pinned her to the spot with his gaze was ice-cold. "Get over this obsession, Lilly. I did not cheat."

She swallowed back the nausea that circled her insides like a shark waiting to pounce. Eight time-lapse photographs didn't lie.

"I want to go."

"Well, we're staying. This is what you signed up for."

She hated him. At that moment she hated him as she'd never hated anyone in her life. "We should never have done this," she murmured huskily. "Look what we're doing to each other."

"We should have done this a long time ago," he disagreed roughly. "My big mistake was giving you time and space when what you really needed was for someone to shake some sense into you."

Her throat tightened. "What does it matter? We're past fixable."

A hard light glittered in his eyes. "That remains to be seen."

"No, it doesn't." She lifted her gaze to his. "This is a short-term solution, Riccardo. You become CEO and we're done."

It was as if her words bounced off his Teflon coating. His expression was inscrutable as he regarded her from beneath lowered lashes. "Matty told me I was a bad husband today."

Her mouth dropped open. "He did?"

"I expect I have been at times."

"At times?" Lilly was past being diplomatic. "That last year you couldn't have cared if I was on Mars as long as I showed up for whatever social function you dictated I appear at. So I could charm the Mayor or sweet-talk a difficult client."

He frowned. "That's an exaggeration. We supported each other. We were a team."

"A team?" She let out a bark of laughter that made a couple near them stare. "If by 'team' you mean I supported you while you ran roughshod over my career every time it was inconvenient for you, then you'd be right."

"Now you're being ridiculous."

"*Really?* You know why I was late that night we had dinner with the owner of Jacob's?" She waited while he paused, then shook his head. "Because I was consulting on the treatment for a little boy's legs. A little boy who'd just lost his mother in a car accident. I was crushed, devastated by what had happened, and all you did when I told you was nod and tell me to get to the table before the appetizers got cold."

"I did *not.* You did not tell me that story."

Her mouth tightened. "Oh, yes, I did. You just couldn't be bothered to listen. And you know what, Riccardo? I helped that little boy. I worked by his side for six months until he was walking again. I might not have been able to bring his mother back but I gave him the use of his legs back. And I'm damn proud of that."

"And so you should be. Lilly, I've always thought what you do is amazing."

"As long as it didn't interfere with the grand plan," she agreed bitterly. "With your obsession to win the CEO job."

A dark flush spread across his cheekbones. "It's my birthright to run De Campo. Why couldn't you ever understand that?"

"I understand it matters to you to the exclusion of everything else in your life. Please forgive me if I don't want to go along for the ride."

A muscle jumped in his jaw. "It won't last forever. Once I'm appointed CEO things will change."

"It'll never change. I think you left a piece of yourself on that racetrack, Riccardo. Nothing you do lives up to that, but you'll never stop looking, *needing* that adrenalin."

The color in his cheeks darkened to a deep, livid red. "Don't try and play psychologist, Lilly. You're not even close."

But she knew she was. She could see it in his face. And finally she felt she was starting to understand him. "Your need for a challenge will always be there. And everyone around you suffers. Our kids would have suffered if we'd been foolish enough to have had them."

"You know that would have changed things."

"No, I don't. We couldn't even keep a dog alive, Riccardo. How would a child have worked?"

The stormclouds in his eyes turned black and dangerous. "That's a ridiculous comparison. Brooklyn was a wild dog. There was nothing we could have done to prevent her death."

She knew he was right. From the day they'd found Brooklyn, a German Shepherd puppy, injured on their street and taken her in, she'd never lost her lust for adventure or for chasing cars.

"You promised you'd train her," she said roughly. "Just like you promised to be around more and you never were."

His mouth flattened into a grim line. "You just can't take your fair share for what happened, can you? You shut me out until I was tired of being verbally slapped in the face every time I walked through the door. And I'm the bad guy for not being around enough? You have a distorted view of the world, Lilly."

The couple beside them suddenly seemed awfully close, their curious gazes on the two of them. Lilly waited until Riccardo had steered them away. "We can talk until we're blue in the face but it isn't going to change the things that were wrong with us."

His fingers tightened around her waist. "Every marriage has its ups and downs. You work through them. You don't run away."

She swallowed hard. If only he knew how badly she'd tried to stick it out. To be what he needed.

His gaze burned into hers, radiating a warning that was impossible to ignore. "We are not over, Lilly."

"We will be in six months."

"And what a six months it's going to be…" He lifted his chin. "Buckle up, *tesoro,* it's going to be quite a ride."

A shiver ran through her. The flicker of the gorgeous two-carat canary-yellow diamond he'd bought to replace the one she'd told him she'd lost shimmered where her hand rested on his shoulder. If he seemed angry now, it would be nothing compared to how he'd react if he knew the truth about what had really happened to the ring.

The organizer of the fashion show waved at her. Her heart lifted to her throat. *She did not want to do this.* The guillotine seemed preferable. But she nodded back at her. The sooner she did this the sooner it was going to be over.

"I have to go."

The tremulous note in her voice drew her husband's eye.

He slid his fingers under her chin and drew her gaze up to his. "What's the matter?"

"Nothing."

"You're nervous."

"I'm not."

She waited for him to release her, but he pulled her closer instead, his eyes flashing as he anchored her against his hard, muscled length. "There was always one way to cure your nerves…"

Lilly started to protest, but he'd already brought his mouth down on hers. His palm cradled her jaw, holding her still while he explored the soft curves of her lips so thoroughly it felt as if he was memorizing them all over again. The heat that flashed between them was undeniable, as life-giving as it had been destructive. She told herself to stop, to end it, but it was impossible not to rise on tiptoes and kiss him back.

No one kissed like Riccardo. No one.

She stepped back, her gaze on his face, wanting him to feel as shaken, as flustered as she was. All she saw was a man still so firmly in control he looked as if he could have been carved out of stone. "Now you have color in your face," he murmured, releasing her and giving her a tap on the behind. "Off you go."

Confused, not sure which way was north and which was south, Lilly did as she was told, following the organizer, Kelly Rankin, to the temporary fitting rooms. Funnily enough, she *did* feel calmer.

Antonia Abelli stripped Lilly down to her underwear. "*Buon Dio,*" she breathed, casting a critical eye over the demure bra and panties Lilly had on. "Really?" She disappeared and came back with flimsy, lacy, non-existent underwear. She told Lilly to put it on. "They're yours. Riccardo will thank me later."

No, he wouldn't. Lilly tried to tell herself that as she closed the curtain on the tiny little changing space and exchanged her own "nothing" underwear for the exquisite lace. This was not a real marriage. And she was definitely not sleeping with Riccardo.

"You need to give me the dress," she told Antonia, peeking around the curtain. "I'm not going out there like this."

The designer whipped the curtain away and gave her a critical look. "You look hot in those."

"Yes, well—" She gasped as Antonia grabbed her arm and yanked her out. Shoulders slumping, cheeks on fire, she stood there, in the middle of all the pre-show chaos, a multitude of mirrors surrounding her, wanting to sink into the floor. Riccardo might have said he liked the changes, but there was too much flesh on her butt for comfort, and too much in her cleavage too, if the truth were told. And her thighs—well, they just looked big. She'd bet five of her extra pounds were *there,* as if she'd reached down and slapped a piece of chocolate cake on them.

"Turn," Antonia ordered, whipping her around with firm hands.

Lilly did her best to ignore all the rail-thin women being dressed around her. But it was hard to because that was her ideal. That was what she thought she *should* look like.

"You have an unrealistic view of your body that has nothing to do with reality." Her therapist's words echoed in her ears. *"You need to change the input you give your brain."*

She tried to look at herself objectively, but it was impossible to concentrate in the middle of a gazillion bodies racing around tucking people in, touching up hair and makeup and waving clipboards. She felt dizzy just watching them. Or was that because her chest felt so tight it was hard to breathe?

One pass down the runway, she told herself, pressing clammy palms together. That was all she had to do.

Antonia pulled the stunning white gown emblazoned with vibrant purple roses over her head and knelt to adjust the hem. Lilly's eyes connected with a hard-looking blond's in the mirror. "Hell," she muttered, her throat tightening. Lacey Craig. Gossip columnist and bitch extraordinaire. The woman who'd begun the end of her marriage.

Lacey sauntered up. "Nice to have you back on the scene."

Why? Because you missed having a punching bag? Lilly looked down at Antonia's updo for fear she might lose it. Lacey had been the worst of the worst when it had come to her and Riccardo's breakup. She'd splashed lurid details—some of them true, some of them not—across the pages of Manhattan's most widely read tabloid. And would have done worse if Lilly hadn't stopped her.

"You might want to watch the weight, though," Lacey commented, running her gaze over her. "Wouldn't want your sexy husband straying again."

Antonia rose to her full five-foot-two inches and nodded at a security guard. "Get her out of here."

Lacey shrugged. "Just a bit of friendly advice. You might have forgotten just how competitive the scene can be."

As if Lilly could ever forget her husband's infidelity. The room swayed around her, the floor tilting under her feet. Perspiration broke out on her forehead and she reached out an arm to steady herself against the wall. It must be a hundred degrees in here...

Antonia grimaced as the security guard ushered Lacey out. "Why can't she ever behave?"

Lilly closed her eyes and told herself to focus. To put the nasty words out of her head and concentrate on getting through this. But visions of those photos flashed through her head like a film strip that wouldn't stop. Riccardo in Chelsea Tate's apartment, standing face-to-face with her in intimate conversation, his dark head bent to hers as he kissed her. Remembering the rest of the blurry series made her stomach churn anew.

Bile rose up in her throat. The sense of betrayal had

been all-consuming. Had sucked her down into a cauldron of self-doubt so deep it had been impossible for her to climb out.

Antonia handed her some water. "Forget that horrible witch," she murmured as she slipped a different pair of shoes on Lilly, then decided she liked Lilly's own better with the dress. "You have a real woman's body that most would die for."

Lilly only barely registered the designer's words. Lost in the world that had destroyed her, she twisted her hands together and stared down at the blindingly beautiful ring on her finger.

The stage manager called for the models. "You need to go," Antonia said. "Keep your head up and don't slouch. I've left the hem a bit long."

She lined up behind the other women at the entrance to the stage, fourth in the queue, but she wasn't really there. All she could see was the brilliant smile on Chelsea Tate's face as she pulled Riccardo in for that kiss.

She ran the back of her hand across her damp forehead. The woman in front of her went out. The show director motioned that she was on.

"Go," he said, giving her a nudge.

She stepped onto the runway. The lights blinded her. The beat of the music pounded in her ears. She started walking, but her legs were shaking so much it was hard to make any progress. The hundreds of faces in rows around the stage were a blur. The long catwalk stretched like an endless sea of white in front of her.

She stumbled, looked down to gauge where she was. Her gaze collided with a handsome blond man sitting in the front row.

Harry.

He smiled at her. She couldn't move her lips out of their frozen curve. Of course he would be here. He worked for the hospital. Her gaze slid down the row to Riccardo, her stomach giving a sickening lurch. *Had they talked to each other?*

She forced herself to keep walking, but her trembling limbs made her misstep again. Her foot slid sideways in her shoe and she stumbled forward. *What the*—? she stuck a desperate hand out to steady herself, but the momentum of her body weight sent her careening off the side of the runway. A choked scream escaped her as the wooden floor rose up to meet her.

Bracing herself for impact, she felt the air hiss from her lungs as a pair of strong arms closed around her and hauled her in.

Winded and dazed, she stared up into the face of Harry Taylor.

"*Hell,* Lilly, are you okay?"

The pounding music made her head spin. The crowd gathering around her was claustrophobic.

She nodded. "I don't know what happened. I—"

"Lilly—" Antonia pushed through the crowd, a horrified look on her face. "I forgot to do up your shoe."

Lilly grimaced and put her hand on Harry's shoulder. "It's okay. I'm fine. You can put—"

"Her down." Riccardo stepped in, his gaze not leaving Harry's face.

No thanks for saving his wife from breaking a few bones. Not even a curt acknowledgement of what he'd done. Her husband stood glaring at Harry, his expression so dark Lilly was convinced most men would have dropped her and run.

But not Harry. He lowered her gently to the floor and held her steady as Antonia knelt and did up her shoe.

"You okay?" he asked again, keeping his hands on her arms until he was sure she had her balance.

Lilly nodded, humiliation washing over her until she wanted to shrivel up into a little droplet of water and disappear between the floorboards.

Kelly Rankin stepped forward. "I am *so* sorry, Lilly," she murmured. "Are you okay to get back up there and continue?"

Riccardo slipped an arm around her waist and pulled her to his side. "She's had enough. Go on without her."

Lilly's humiliation degenerated into a slow, explosive burn. He had been the one to make her do this. He had insisted on her doing something she clearly wasn't comfortable with. *How dared he act so concerned?*

If she didn't get back up there and hold her head high she would never get over it. Pressing her lips together, she turned to Kelly. "I'm fine. Let's do it."

The organizer gave her a relieved look and went backstage. Harry stepped back and went to his seat. Lilly went on tiptoe and put her mouth to Riccardo's ear. "Never, *ever* speak for me in public again."

Then she turned and followed Antonia, leaving her stunned husband staring after her.

"Good for you, getting back up there."

An attractive fifty-something brunette gave Lilly an encouraging smile as she touched up her lipstick in the ladies' room. "I'm not sure I would have."

Lilly flashed her a polite smile. "Not much else I could do."

The woman shrugged and tossed her perfume in her purse. "Well, you looked gorgeous. I hope you get to keep the dress."

She did, in fact. Riccardo had it outside, in a monogrammed Antonia Abelli bag that also held her own less-than-spectacular underwear. Although she doubted she'd ever wear the dress again. Not after tonight. Not after she'd crashed and burned so spectacularly in it.

She nodded at the woman and left. No less than a dozen people had come up to her since the show had ended. It would have been more if Riccardo hadn't acted as gate-keeper.

Her husband's mood had gone steeply downhill since she'd ended up in Harry's arms, and she'd been relieved at his suggestion they leave shortly after. Determined to avoid as many people as she could, she walked around the edge of the crowd toward the entrance.

"Lilly."

Harry Taylor stood in front of her, a determined look on his face.

"I wanted to make sure you're okay."

She smiled and gave him a kiss on the cheek. "More embarrassed than anything. Thank you for rescuing me."

His gaze sharpened on her face. "You sure? You looked like a ghost up there—not like yourself at all."

She nodded. "I'm fine, really. Just tired. We're leaving now."

He pulled at his tie and gave her a pained look. "You know I meant what I said the other day. I don't think Riccardo is the right guy for you. And I'm always here if you need me."

Lilly bit her lip. "Look, I shouldn't be talking to you, Harry—Riccardo will hit the roof."

"That's exactly what I mean," he pointed out, frowning. "Why should you have to worry about that? Dammit, Lilly, if that bastard starts treating you badly I swear I will—"

"What?"

She spun around to find her husband standing behind them, a barely restrained look of violence on his face.

"What will you do, Taylor? I'd like to know."

Harry stepped forward. He wasn't a short man, but Riccardo had three inches on him easily. That didn't seem to faze Harry as he stood toe to toe with him. "I will hold you accountable."

Riccardo gave him a silky look. "My wife and I and our

personal life are none of your business. Accept the fact that you never stood a chance, Taylor."

Harry's face turned bright red. Lilly stared as a man who never lost control balled his hand into a fist and sent it arcing toward her husband's face. Riccardo's reflexes, honed by years as a competitive athlete, were lightning-fast and he caught the other man's wrist in his hand before it connected.

Light exploded around them. Lilly looked up to see a half-dozen cameras pointed at them. *Oh, my God.* How could this be happening?

"Guys," she pleaded, pulling on Riccardo's arm. "Stop."

Her husband dropped his hand away but stayed toe to toe with Harry. "You come near my wife again and I will take you apart piece by piece."

Harry lifted his chin. "You don't scare me, De Campo. You—"

"Harry!" Lilly had the hysterical thought that if he'd acted more like *this*—more manly, more aggressive—he might have done it for her. She took a deep breath and gave both men a level look. "We are leaving. Goodnight, Harry."

Riccardo drove home like he was on a racecourse instead of in the middle of Manhattan, and was shocked when no police officer appeared to pull him over. Lilly was out of the car and flouncing up the walkway before he came to a complete stop in their driveway, but she'd forgotten he was the only one with keys and had to cool her heels while he parked and strolled leisurely up to the door. She stood back while he inserted his key and pushed it open, then swept by him, her head held high, fury in her hazel eyes. Her heels clicked on the hardwood floor as she charged upstairs without another word.

His own safety valve about to blow, he walked into his study and poured himself a Scotch. *"I don't think Riccardo is the right guy for you..."* Taylor's smug pronouncement:

"I'm always here if you need me." His blood burned in his veins, snaking through him like a river of fire. Taylor was there in the wings, waiting for her. Waiting for *him* to screw up. And what had he done to deserve it?

He took a swig of Scotch and stifled the urge to go back there and finish Taylor off. *He* was the only man Lilly was ever going to run to. He knew it and she knew it.

It was time he proved it to her.

He downed the Scotch in two gulps, slammed the glass down on the sideboard and took the stairs to their bedroom two at a time. When he arrived in the doorway Lilly was standing in front of the closet, her shoes in her hands. He sucked in a breath. She had taken her dress off and stood there in a very sexy, very skimpy lacy white panties and bra.

Desire slammed into him, hot and hard.

Lilly flicked her gaze over him, her cat eyes wary and defiant. "Get out."

He shook his head and leaned back against the door frame. "I don't think so."

Her eyes grew larger—big, bottomless pools of amber and green he could lose himself in. Her spine stiffened as she turned fully to face him. She was afraid of him, and with a savage inner growl he acknowledged that he didn't care.

He moved toward her, his steps slow and purposeful. "I warned you not to talk to him."

She planted her hands on her hips. "I fell off that runway because *you* insisted I model that dress. Harry just wanted to see if I was okay."

His mouth twisted. "He wanted to remind you he's still around."

"Good thing he was, or who would have caught me?"

She knew her mistake the minute he stepped in to trap her against the door. "You think I'm never there for you, Lilly? Well, here I am."

He could hear her agitated breathing, see the confusion and fire that swirled in her eyes. "Go to hell," she blazed, her shoulders pressing back into the door.

"I'd rather go down on you," he murmured, sliding the back of his hand over her rosy cheek. "I know how sweet you taste, *tesoro*. How much you love it when I— Ah—" He caught the hand she swung at him and twisted it behind her back. "Don't do that."

She bit out a curse and fought against his hold, but he held her firm. "Dammit, Riccardo, let me go."

He dropped her hand and stepped in closer, until his body was pushed up against hers. "Time to talk in the only way we know how."

She squirmed against him as he imprinted her with *his* brand of honesty—the hard, throbbing truth of his lust, which was quickly sending him over the edge. But she wasn't being very convincing and he could hear how her breathing had quickened.

"Give it up, Lilly," he murmured, lowering his mouth to hers. "We both know how this is going to end."

She said something against his lips and he replied with a hard, bruising kiss that was about control, not pleasure. She'd always liked it when he dominated, and he knew that hadn't changed.

She pressed her lips mutinously shut as he slid his tongue against the crease and demanded entry. Smiling at that, he trailed his hand down over the newly voluptuous curves of her breasts, over the nipple that jutted through the lacy material that covered her, and rolled the hard nub between his fingers. She made a sound low in her throat and twisted against him, but it wasn't the movement of a woman who wanted to go anywhere. Her eyes were closed and her lips had softened, and when he swept his thumb over the hard tip and made it come to full erectness she sagged against him.

Melted into him.

He buried his hands in the thick swath of hair at the nape of her neck. Then he kissed her again, and this time she opened for him and let him take the kiss deeper, into an achingly intimate caress that told her exactly what he wanted to do to her with his tongue and with his body.

The broken sound that came from her throat told him the battle had been won.

"*Basta*," he murmured. "Enough denying ourselves what we both want."

Lilly pressed her hands back against the door as he ran his palm down the trembling flatness of her stomach. "Ric—"

He slid his hand underneath the silk that covered her and his fingers delved into the hot cleft between her thighs. She gasped and arched against his hand. A primal surge of heat flashed through him. She was wet—oh, so wet for him— and he nearly lost it right there. But he savagely yanked back his control and stilled his fingers to growl, "Tell me you love it when I touch you, *tesoro*."

She nodded, but kept her eyes shut.

"Say it."

"Dammit, yes. Please—"

"And I'm the only man who's ever going to touch you like this?"

She moaned her assent. Satisfied, he slid his fingers against the warm silk of her and indulged his craving to touch her in every way possible.

Her sudden intake of breath and her hands against his chest took him off guard.

"Get your hands off me."

He drew back. "Lil—"

"That's what this is about, isn't it?" Her voice rose in furious accusation. "Control. *You* being the only one to ever have me. *Me* doing what you want."

He frowned. "You were as into that as I was."

"I was being stupid. *Stupid.* How could I forget what this

is all about? You—always you, Riccardo." She pushed her hair out of her face. "Claiming what's yours."

"You're being ridiculous."

Her eyes glittered. "No, I've finally got my head back. Lord forbid *I* forget to keep my eye on the prize. You certainly haven't."

He shook his head. "What are you talking about?"

"I am not something to be conquered," she said thickly. "I am your wife. You just can't understand that."

"Lilly—"

"Get out." Her face was a blotchy patchwork of red. "Get out or I will walk out of here and never come back, deal or no deal."

Deciding there was no reasoning with her while she was in this state, he turned on his heel and left, hearing the door slam behind him.

He took a cold shower in the guest bedroom, letting the freezing water pound down on his shoulders. *Was* he demented for even attempting this plan of his? To want to make Lilly pay for everything she'd done to him? The humiliation she'd caused him? Because he wasn't sure who was winning—her or him.

CHAPTER SIX

"*THIS IS YOUR* idea of convincing the board you're the man to lead De Campo?"

Gabe shoved a folded newspaper under Riccardo's nose.

He sat back in his office chair and glanced at the tabloid. It was the same one Lilly had waved in his face this morning on her way to work. Having the juiciest of all the coverage of the charity event, it sported the headline "Trouble in Paradise—Already?", which was set over a montage of three photos of him and Lilly laid out in timeline fashion.

The first was of him kissing her on the dance floor. He studied it critically. They *looked* very much in love, despite the fact they hadn't talked in days. The second was of Lilly falling off the runway into Taylor's arms. His mouth tightened. *That* he'd like to forget. The third was a shot of himself restraining the surgeon after he'd thrown that punch.

All in all, fairly damaging.

"What can I say?" He shrugged. "It's a slow news day."

Gabe lifted a brow at him. "What the hell happened? Fisticuffs aren't usually your style—although lately I have to say you're doing a pretty good job of it."

Riccardo spread his fingers in an expressive gesture. "He threw a punch."

Gabe sat on the edge of his desk. "Why?"

"He cornered Lilly and made it clear he was going to

be around to pick up the pieces when I broke her heart. I took offense at that."

His brother let out a low whistle. "I'm surprised you didn't slug him."

"That would have been giving the board far too much ammunition."

"And Lilly falling off the runway?"

"The designer forgot to do up her shoe."

"You're kidding?"

He crumpled up the paper and tossed it freethrow-style into the garbage can he kept across the room for exactly that purpose. "She was a trooper. She got right back up there and did it again."

"That's Lilly." His brother grinned. "She has *spirito*."

Until the end. When she'd become a shadow of her former self. When she'd had that same look on her face she'd had before going up on that stage *every* night before they'd gone out. As if she'd been dreading it.

A wave of remorse settled over him. He'd been the son-of-a-bitch who'd made her go up there. And, even though he had no idea what had set her off, it had been wrong to do it.

Dio. He picked up his coffee and glowered into it. Lilly had used to be comfortable in the center of it all. They'd been nicknamed the Golden Couple for their ability to work a room.

So what had changed?

She had accused him of never being there for her. The symbolic act of Taylor rescuing her and not him had been a brutal shot to his ego. Not just because he'd been five feet away and Taylor had sprung out of his seat like Sir Galahad on a white steed. But because it had once again reinforced the fact that she'd left him. That he wasn't the one she wanted. The fact that he had no clue *who* she really was.

His hand tightened around the coffee cup, red-hot anger slicing through him. It was time he and Lilly had a long conversation about a lot of things—not the least of which was what had really happened to her during those last few months of their marriage. Why she'd frozen him out. Become a ghost of who she'd been. It had to be about more than Chelsea. And he was sure that last night held the key to at least some of it.

Gabe glanced at his watch. "You ready?"

Riccardo nodded.

The cold war between him and Lilly couldn't go on forever. Not with this battle with the board and his father ahead of him. Not when he was intent on claiming what was rightfully his. Both at home and in the boardroom.

There was a knock on the door. He got to his feet as Paige, his PA, came in.

"The meeting's about to start."

He nodded and slipped on his jacket. It was possibly the most important meeting of his life, in which he was to lay out his plans for De Campo's future to the board, and here he was obsessing over his wife. His mouth twisted. Lilly would find that bitterly amusing, he was sure.

He picked up his laptop and followed Gabe out of the room.

"Ah…Riccardo?" Paige lifted a brow at him as he walked past her.

"Mmm?"

"Want the blueprints?"

The blueprints of their new restaurant in SoHo. The centerpiece of his presentation. He grimaced and took them from her. "What would I do without you?"

Antonio had the same salacious tabloid Riccardo had now seen twice this morning tucked in front of him when they walked into the room. Riccardo swept his gaze around the table. So did Phil Bedford and Chase Kenyon. *Hell*. Was his life a walking soap opera?

"Smoothing the way, I see," his father murmured as he

took his place beside him. "Did you know Phil Bedford plays golf with Harry Taylor?"

Riccardo deposited his laptop on the table with slightly more force than was necessary, picked up his father's paper and waved it in the air. "Looks like most of you have seen the paper this morning?"

Matty's mouth dropped open. Gabe looked fascinated. All the other extremely senior heads of their corporations sat there silently and stared at him. He shifted his gaze to Phil Bedford, the portly CEO of a consumer packaged goods company pushing fifty.

"Harry Taylor wants to date my wife. I don't consider that a valid proposition since she is *still* my wife. So I acted on it." He threw the paper down on the table like the trash it was and eyed the room. "If anyone would like to crucify me with this please do so now, so we can get on with business."

Phil Bedford stared down at his coffee. Chase Kenyon doodled on his notepad.

"Fine." Riccardo looked at Antonio. "All yours."

He could have sworn his father was holding back laughter as he got to his feet and opened the meeting. Antonio gave a holistic presentation on how the De Campo Group was performing worldwide, every bit the elegant global wine baron as he talked through the slides in his thick accent, then turned the meeting over to Riccardo for an update on the restaurant business.

Riccardo opened with an overview of the division's strong growth prospects, then ran through a presentation on the new jewel in the De Campo restaurant crown—Zambia, the SoHo restaurant set to open in six months. He saw the lights go on in the board members' eyes as he spoke of the twelve percent overall profit increase the restaurant division would bring in, and knew he'd driven home his message of where the future was for De Campo.

He sat down, his jaw clenched with satisfaction. He had nailed it.

Gabe stood to give an update on the California operations. Another board member gave a presentation on how lessons learned from the packaged goods industry could be applied to wine. Then they broke for lunch.

Antonio followed him into his office. *"Buon lavoro, figlio."*

Good job, son.

Caught off-guard by the compliment, he warily inclined his head. *"Grazie."*

"You keep this up and I might just throw my weight behind you."

He froze. *The son-of-a-bitch.* Even after the results he'd just presented Antonio was still stringing him along.

He dragged in a breath and let it out slowly. "I will be single-handedly responsible for that twelve percent profit you just gloated over. You start putting recognition where it's due or so, help me God, I will leave this company and not look back."

His father set his chin at that haughty angle he favored. "A De Campo would *never* utter those words."

"This one just did." Riccardo jammed his hands in his pockets and paced to the window. "Just out of curiosity, how long do you intend to make me pay?"

Antonio narrowed his gaze on him. "Is that what you think I'm doing?"

"I *know* that's what you're doing."

"Maybe I think Gabe would do a better job."

He stiffened, white-hot rage slicing through him. "We are not Cain and Abel, with you playing God, Antonio. I will *not* compete with my brother. Make a decision, but do not try and drive a wedge between us. Neither of us will tolerate it."

His father shrugged his broad shoulders. "Some think Gabe has the true love for this business. He's aggressive, with just the right amount of conservatism."

"Then why didn't you choose him to run the company while you were ill? You had the opportunity."

Antonio met his combative stare with one of his own. "Because, despite the fact that you dishonored this family by choosing a racing career over your heritage, you have the heart of a lion, Riccardo. You have the vision to take this company where it needs to go."

"So does Gabe."

His father shook his head. "Not like you. You have the ability to be brutal. To make the decisions no one else wants to make."

"Then do it," Riccardo gritted out. "Because I'm not waiting much longer. I've sacrificed too much."

Antonio pointed a beefy finger at him. "How long have I been waiting to hear you say that?"

Riccardo frowned. "What?"

"Sacrifice. You view De Campo as a sacrifice. As an impediment to your personal freedom. Not as the majestic birthright that's been handed to you."

"I love this company. I have killed myself for this company. I do *not* view it as a sacrifice. But I *have* sacrificed for it." He trained his gaze on his father. "As you did."

"Prove it." His father flicked his hand in the air in a dismissive motion. "I'm retiring in three months. The job is yours to lose."

"You might just kill me one of these days."

The big, burly football player wiped the sweat from his face and stepped off the treadmill. Lilly smiled and made a note of the time in her chart. What would normally have been a walk-in-the-park run for Trent Goodman had been a one-mile endurance test on a knee that had a whole lot of healing ahead before he stepped back on a football field.

"Admit it—you like coming to see me."

"Are you kidding?" He dropped the towel in his bag and slung it over his shoulder. "It's the highlight of my week.

The pain I can take, when I'm getting the inside scoop on all the gossip. You get more press than I do—and frankly," he admitted sheepishly, "that's not a good thing."

Lilly laughed. "Believe me—I'd happily pass it along if I could."

"I bet you would." He grinned. "That photo of your husband tangling with the doctor? Priceless."

Maybe somewhat less than priceless. She was now back as a fixture in all the gossip rags. She'd spent the weekend fuming at Riccardo's caveman tactics. Both with Harry and in the bedroom.

"He has his moments," she murmured, looking back at the clipboard. "Same time tomorrow?"

He nodded and blew her a kiss. She smiled and watched him leave. Muscular, gorgeous, charming and making millions…Trent would have had most women on their knees with his overt flirtatiousness. Lilly, however, was fixated on her own brutish male.

What in the world had gotten into her? She'd nearly toppled. Slept with him and done something she'd have sorely regretted. All because she still couldn't keep her hands to herself when it came to Riccardo.

She twirled a chunk of hair around her finger. They had exchanged a total of about a hundred words since that scene in the bedroom. If he was in the kitchen when she came down, she took her coffee onto the patio. If she came down first, he went and watched the news in his study.

It couldn't go on like this.

Unresolved issues lay between them like unexploded mines. Yet Saturday night had proved beyond a shadow of a doubt she never wanted to live the life of Riccardo's society wife ever again. That she'd been right to leave when she had.

That she wasn't *capable* of living it beyond the six months she'd committed to.

So why did everything feel so wrong? Why couldn't

she just do what she needed to in public and to hell with how things were at home? She tossed her clipboard on her desk and grabbed the notes on her afternoon patients so she could file them. She had pushed a set of notes into a folder and slid it back into the drawer before realizing she'd completely mixed the two patients up. *Damn.* She pulled the two folders out again.

A loud piano piece filled the air. She frowned. *Her new ringtone.* Note to self: change that. She pulled her phone out of her pocket and held it to her ear while she fixed the notes.

"Lilly Anderson."

"De Campo," Riccardo's rich drawl oozed across the line. "Really, Lilly, you have to get with the program."

"I don't use your name professionally. You know that."

"I don't like it. I'm calling to ask your permission to ask Katy to clear your schedule for Thursday and Friday."

Her husband's drily delivered request made Lilly frown and push the drawer of the filing cabinet shut with her foot. Riccardo asking for her permission to do something? Was he sick? On some type of mood-altering medication?

She cleared her throat and chose her words carefully. "I have clinics at the hospital on Thurdsay and Friday. Is it important?"

"I'd like to take you to Barbados for the weekend."

"The Caribbean island of Barbados?"

"The one and only," he confirmed, amusement lacing his tone. "A friend of mine offered up his place for the weekend."

She stuck a finger in her mouth and chewed on her nail. "So it's a business thing?"

"No." His voice deepened to that silky tone that made her toes squish in her shoes. "Definitely not business."

Heat filled her cheeks. "Riccardo—"

He sighed. "We need a truce. We need to talk, Lil. Somewhere by ourselves, with no photographers, no one interrupting us, neither of us rushing off to work… Just us."

She couldn't deny that. It was just that it sounded sort of…*terrifying.* She rested her hip on the corner of the desk and the guilty thought came to her that maybe, *maybe,* if she'd talked to him from the start instead of shutting down things *would* have been different.

A snapping sound filled the air. She pulled her finger out of her mouth and stared, horrified, at her broken nail. She hadn't bitten her nails in exactly twelve months.

"You still there?"

"Yes."

Another sigh. "I'm pretending I'm asking, but I'm not really, you know."

She smiled. At least she knew her husband hadn't been abducted by aliens. She stared down at her wreck of a nail and swallowed hard. "To be clear—this is a discussion? That's all?"

"A discussion," he agreed firmly. "That's all I'm asking for."

"Okay, then, yes." It would be closure for them both.

"Good. Will you tell Katy or will I?"

"I will."

"*Bene.* I'm off for dinner with the boys and Antonio." His voice took on a sardonic edge. "Wish me luck."

"Keep your cool. You'll be fine."

A meaningful silence came down the phone line. "Already lost it. *Ciao, bella.*"

"*Ciao.*"

Lilly pressed the end button, her skin tingling from the effects of those two softly spoken words. Would there ever come a day when *that* didn't make her want to throw caution to the wind and do exactly what she wasn't supposed to do?

She fought the sinking feeling she had just made a huge mistake and dialed her sister.

Alex answered with a distracted, "Hello."

"It's your sister. Got a sec?"

"Always. How are you holding up? Riccardo mix it up with anyone lately?"

"Very funny." Lilly pulled a pristine nail out of her mouth before she trashed that one too. "We have to re-schedule brunch. I'm going to be away this weekend."

"What lifestyle-of-the-rich-and-famous event is he tak-ing you to?"

"None. We're going to Barbados together."

"*Damn. I* would put up with him for a weekend like that."

Lilly smiled. "Gabe's still in town, you know."

"Mmm, yes—well, I'm afraid I'm not up for twenty-four-seven sparring. Dr. Overlea just called to say he's scheduled Lisbeth in for some pretreatments next week. I'm going to head home and keep her company so she doesn't stress."

Lilly's throat tightened. "I didn't think he was going to be able to get her in so soon."

"He needs to do this before he schedules treatment with the clinic in Switzerland."

"Right." She swallowed hard. "I—" *Hell.* The conver-sation with Riccardo was important, but her sister's health was more so.

"Lil—it's fine. I'll go." Her sister's voice softened. "You guys need time together."

She chewed on her lip. Alex probably thought she and Riccardo were having hot reunion sex every night… She so desperately wanted to tell her that, no, they weren't, that they were hardly talking to each other and she was hope-lessly confused, but she couldn't. Not if she was to keep her and Riccardo's deal.

"You'll call me if you need me? I'll come right back."

"I will. I promise."

Her shoulders sagged. "Okay."

"By the way—one of the girls here just showed me some

of the stuff the tabloids are saying about you. Please tell me you're not reading it?"

"I'm not reading it." Only a bit. One or two particularly horrid pieces…

"Yes, you are. I can tell. You have to stop it, Lil. It's awful, destructive stuff and not a bit true. I've never seen you looking so good."

Lilly sighed. "I'm fine, Alex. I promise." Only her sister knew how deep her body issues went and she called her on it when she needed to.

"You sure?"

"I gave my whole wardrobe to charity," she said drily. "Riccardo almost had a fit."

"The whole thing?" her sister squeaked.

"All of it."

"I can't tell you how glad I am to hear you say that."

"I know… Al?"

"Yeah?"

"Do you really think people never change?"

She sighed. "Are you talking about Riccardo?"

"Yes."

And why, exactly, was she?

Her sister cleared her throat. "When we were looking at those tabloids this morning, one of the girls here looked at that photo of you and Riccardo kissing—which is dreamy, by the way, and I don't *do* dreamy, as you know—and she got this stupid, expression on her face and said, 'I just want *that*. To be that much in love.'"

Lilly felt the stitches she'd triple-sewed around her heart rip, leaving it jagged and raw. *She* wanted to be that much in love again. But that wasn't her and Riccardo anymore, and telling herself that was possible was foolish.

"So," her sister continued, "while I think he might be the most arrogant son-of-a-bitch I've ever met, I know what you have is special, Lil, and that man is crazy about you in his own demented way. Which leads me to believe he's going to do whatever it takes to keep you."

Lilly stood there, wishing she'd never asked the question in the first place.

"Do me a favor?" Alex's voice lost its sarcasm and took on a serious note.

"Name it."

"Whatever you do, don't get pregnant."

Lilly stared at the phone, horrified. Then remembered her sister didn't know. Didn't know this was all a charade. "Of course I won't. That would complicate everything."

"Exactly."

Exactly. She glanced at her watch. "I'm done for the day, and Riccardo's out with the boys. You up to swimsuit-shopping? You're the only one I know who'll give me an honest opinion."

They made arrangements to meet and Lilly hung up, more worried with every passing moment that a "conversation" in Barbados with her sexier than hell husband was a disaster waiting to happen.

One thing she knew for sure. She could never, never tell him about why she'd entered into this deal. About Lisbeth. Because she didn't trust him not to use that against her. And Lisbeth was all that mattered.

CHAPTER SEVEN

LILLY STOOD ON the patio of Charles Greene's very beautiful, very exclusive Barbados estate overlooking Heron Bay.
The sparkling, water-soaked playground of the world's rich
and famous, the bay was dotted with luxury hotels and vil-
las that sat on heavenly golden sand beaches and the most
stunning clear turquoise water Lilly had ever seen.

If you were the world's most famous golfer you took
over Heron Bay's five-thousand-dollar-a-night marquee
hotel for a sunset marriage featuring heads of state, rock
stars and movie icons. If you were Charles Greene, Brit-
ish billionaire and heir to a heavy machinery fortune, you
bought this gorgeous six-bedroom villa on the ocean and
kept it for yourself.

Charles and Riccardo had done business together on a
few occasions, and had formed a close personal relationship in addition to their working one. With Charles away
on business in the UK, the villa was theirs. A private oasis
in paradise.

At any other time in her life Lilly would have been ec-
static to be here. But not tonight. Not when she was about
to learn the truth about her marriage.

She kept her feet planted firmly on the concrete. Tonight
was not about running. It was about facing her demons.

She drank in the sheet of shimmering perfect blue sea
in front of her, its color morphing from light to dark tur-

quoise, then to a marine blue the further out the eye traveled. Were relationships like that? she wondered. Were there gradations and depths she and Riccardo had yet to explore? Or would this be the end for them?

"I'm leaving now."

Mrs. Adams, the housekeeper who had greeted them and shown them to their rooms, appeared on the patio with a bottle of wine and a cooler in her hands. "Mr. De Campo thought you might enjoy a glass of wine while he showers."

Lilly forced a smile to her lips. "Thank you. He's off the phone, then?"

She nodded. "He said to tell you he'd be down in a few minutes." She set the cooler down on the table and took some glasses out of a cupboard. "Did you say you'd been here before?"

"Yes. A year ago."

Riccardo had come here on business and brought her with him. It had been right after news of his affair had surfaced and she'd spent the whole week trying to convince herself she shouldn't doubt him. Trying to save her marriage.

Until she'd seen the photos.

"It's a beautiful island," she murmured, realizing the woman was waiting for her response. "We stayed further up the coast."

Her brief response had the desired effect. The housekeeper nodded and stuck her hands on her hips. "I'll be back tomorrow to cook breakfast. Would you like me to pour you a glass of wine?"

"No, thank you. I can pour it."

"Okay, see you tomorrow, then."

"Goodnight."

Lilly kept the plastic smile on her face until the housekeeper had disappeared into the house. Her body vibrated with a tension that hadn't left her since they'd climbed aboard the De Campo jet and flown the five hours south to the island—a flight the entire duration of which Riccardo had worked. She pulled in a breath to steady herself, but the shallow pulls of air she managed to take in didn't help much.

She turned back to the sea and laced her hands together. *"Stay in the moment. Allow yourself to feel and move through the pain..."* Her therapist's words were a grounding force when all she wanted to do was run. It had been her coping mechanism since she was a teenager and her parents had been having their no-holds-barred fights to run when she was in pain. To refuse to feel it.

Making herself stand here was like being asked to walk over red-hot coals.

"You haven't had any wine."

Riccardo's low, smooth observation contrasted sharply with the imminent hysteria she felt building within her. This had always been the pattern with them. Him handling everything with reason—with well-thought-out premeditation. Lilly shooting from the hip—driven by emotion.

She turned around, a sharp condemnation on her lips. But he was so breathtakingly handsome in jeans and a navy polo shirt, his square-jawed, dark good looks only intensified by the casual attire, that the words fled her head.

He was beautiful beyond the meaning of the word. Charisma oozed out of him like oxygen for the female race. And she knew then that this had been a big, huge mistake.

Just as it had been to think she could claim ownership over a man every woman wanted.

She turned back to look at the ocean. "You can pour me some now."

The knot in her stomach grew to an almost incapacitating level as she heard him walk across the patio and pour the wine. The sound of bubbling liquid hitting glass was deafeningly loud on the night air.

He came to stand beside her, the smoky, spicy scent of him wrapping itself around her.

"What's wrong?"

She swiveled to face him. "You've been talking on that phone non-stop since we left. I thought we had a no work rule."

His mouth tightened. "It's off now. I just had a few last things to go through with Gabe. By the way," he added, raising a brow, "he asked Alex out for dinner and she turned him down flat. Said she was going back to Mason Hill for the weekend." His gaze narrowed on her face. "You two *never* go home. Is everything okay with your family?"

She blanched. "Everything's fine. Can we just get this over with?"

He kept that watchful dark gaze on her. Then handed her the glass of wine.

She wrapped her fingers around the stem. The glass shook in her hand.

"Lil—" His eyes moved from her shaking fingers to her face.

"I'm fine," she murmured. "You—you start."

He exhaled harshly, the nostrils of his perfectly straight Roman nose flaring.

"What happened the night of the fashion show? Why were you so afraid to do it?"

She blinked. She had not expected that to be his first question. "You know I've never been comfortable in that type of setting. I told you that when we first started dating."

"But you got over it. You thrived on it."

"I hated every minute of it. I trained myself to do it so I wouldn't let you down."

Confusion flickered in his eyes. "Why? Why would a woman like you have confidence issues? You had the position, the wealth, the looks to back you. Why would you feel inferior?"

She gave a twisted smile. "I come from a town of two thousand, five hundred people, Riccardo. I will always feel small-town, no matter how you dress me up or how many places you take me or how many etiquette rules you teach me." She shook her head. "You swept me up into this glamorous life I had no coping skills for, tossed me into the deep end and expected me to swim."

He frowned. "But you never said anything. To me— you were just fine."

Her shoulders stiffened. "I was doing what I had to do. That was my *job*. My role as Lilly De Campo."

He exhaled heavily. "No one would ever have known you felt that way."

Her lips twisted in a bitter smile. "I became extraordinarily good at faking it. And why not? I faked my way through our entire marriage."

His gaze sharpened on her face, a dangerous glint firing in its dark depths. "I think you'd better explain that."

"I never wanted that life, Riccardo. I told you that when you knocked me off my feet in that bar in SoHo. But you wouldn't listen…you kept pushing until I said yes."

"We were in love with each other," he growled.

"We were infatuated with each other," she corrected. "There was still time to recognize how wrong it was for me. How self-destructive all the attention and criticism was."

"How so?"

She set her wine down on the railing and pushed her hair behind her ears. "I've never been secure in the way I look. It's always been a tough one for me. But as your wife I couldn't put on five pounds without the tabloids noticing and pouncing on me."

"I told you. Stop reading them."

"That's overly simplistic. They were everywhere. I couldn't avoid them all."

His brows drew together. "But where does it come from, then, this insecurity about your looks? Beyond what the tabloids say?"

She turned away from his penetrating barrage of questions. But her therapist's words haunted her, refused to let her back away. *"Above all be honest, Lilly. Be honest with yourself and those around you."*

She took a deep breath. "I was very unhappy as a teenager. My parents' marriage was a mess for a long time. The farm wasn't doing well and the stress of having no money was getting to them. The kids—we had no life. We spent all our time helping out on the farm. We barely had time for schoolwork, let alone social lives."

"I knew you weren't happy at home and that's why you left," he said quietly. "But I didn't know it was that bad."

She nodded. "My parents' fights would dissolve into screaming matches. Plates would fly and my mother would threaten to leave. My dad had an affair with the farmer's wife down the road." She hugged her arms around herself and looked up at him. "It was a disaster. A huge mess."

There was a pregnant silence. His face paled. *Yes,* she thought viciously. *That's why what you did hurt so much.*

She kept going, afraid that if she stopped she'd never tell him the truth. "David seemed immune to it all. Lisbeth was too young to know what was happening. Alex dealt with it by getting into trouble—running with the wrong crowd. I internalized it. I thought if I could control everything about my life beyond them, beyond what was happening at home, I'd be okay."

Her mouth felt wooden, her lips thick, and the desire to stop talking was so strong it was hard to make herself form the words. "My big thing was food. I hated the way I looked so I controlled everything I put in my mouth." She swallowed hard. "To the point where I was hardly eating."

His eyes darkened with an emotion she couldn't read. "But you can't ever have been fat. Why in the world would you hate yourself so much?"

"I was a 'chunky, healthy, solid-boned farmgirl,' as my mother would say," she said with a derisive smile. "And I hated it. No one wanted to date me. No one wanted to be with me."

"I find that hard to believe."

"It wasn't until I was in my twenties that I bloomed. Came into myself. You met me not long after that."

He frowned. "So why is it still so bad? I've seen men lust after you, Lilly. You know they do. That must give you some confidence."

"Yes." She turned back to look at the brilliant sunset staining the sky now, the giant ball of orange and red sinking into the horizon. She swallowed past the hard, round mass in her throat that felt as if it was choking her, as if revealing her shameful secret might bring her to her knees. "But not before I developed anorexia."

There was a long silence. He scraped his hand over his jaw and stared at her. "I had no idea."

She made a face. "It's not something you drop into casual conversation, like the fact I had a dog named Honey when I was little."

"*Dio,* Lilly." He stepped forward and took her by the shoulders. "That's not what I'm talking about. This is key to who you are. Essential information I need to know about you. I would never have put you through any of this if I'd known that."

She lifted her chin. "I didn't want you to know."

"Why?" He threw up his hands. "Because for once I might see who the real Lilly De Campo is?"

"No, I—"

"Lilly, we've been as intimate as two people can be. We've spent hours devouring each other. Yet you still can't tell me these profound truths about yourself? No wonder we're messed up."

She shook her head and took a step back. "Sex and intimacy are two different things."

"They most certainly are," he agreed tightly. "And the minute you turned into the Ice Queen and froze me out any intimacy we had was blown to bits."

She winced. "I wasn't trying to hurt you. I was trying

to protect myself. My anorexia was my deep, dark secret. It was the thing no one knew about me in my new life. The thing I never wanted anyone to know about me. Most of all you."

A muscle jumped in his jaw. "Why?"

She pressed her lips together. "You're a perfect human being, Riccardo. Everything about you is so damn perfect that everyone wants you, everyone admires you. I've never felt I could live up to it. *Be* that woman who's worthy of you."

"That's ridiculous."

She stamped her foot. "*It's how I feel, dammit.* Everything—*everything* about my life with you was about keeping up appearances. Making sure we were that Golden Couple. And the balance I'd tried so hard to inject into my life in order to stay healthy went out the window. How could it not when I was constantly in the spotlight? Constantly being judged?"

He raked his hand through his hair. "I wish you'd told me so I could have helped you."

Her heart throbbed in her chest. "I didn't want to add myself to your list of issues. You had enough going on with De Campo business."

He shook his head. "Did *I* ever put any pressure on you about your weight?"

"You never reassured me."

"I *always* told you how gorgeous you looked."

"Yes, but when I said things like, 'I feel fat,' to get some reassurance from you, you told me to go to the gym."

"That's because that's what *I* do when I feel like that. I work out, get the tension out, and I feel better about myself. *Hell,* Lilly…" He was staring at her as if she was a creature from another planet. "Has there ever been any doubt about how much I love your body?"

Her gaze skipped away from his. "I've put on weight since we were together."

"And that scene the other night wasn't enough to convince you I like the changes?"

"Why wasn't I enough, then?" She yelled the words at him, her control snapping. "If you think I'm beautiful, if I'm *enough* for you, then why did you have to have an affair with Chelsea Tate?"

All the color drained out of his face. "It didn't happen. You're the only woman I want, Lilly. Chelsea never came close to meaning anything like that to me."

"*Then tell me the truth,*" she raged, pointing a finger at him. "This is my life, Riccardo. Not a tabloid page. When I left you I was in the fetal position for three days. *Three days.* And if Alex hadn't come along to dig me out I might still be there. So do *not* tell me any more lies. I can't take it."

He stared at her with the glazed look of a man who didn't know where to go. What to do. She watched him take a deep breath and steady himself and felt her heart sink into the depths of hell.

"You need to give me a chance to explain…"

She bit back the bile that rose in her throat. "Believe me—you have my full attention."

He raked a hand through his hair and set his jaw. "Chelsea and I were once close—you know that. But once I met you that all ended and you were the only woman in my life. The *only* one, Lilly." He frowned when she gave no reaction. "When things got so bad between us I was completely at a loss as to what to do. It was impossible to believe a marriage could go from one-fifty to zero in a matter of months—but somehow ours did, and I couldn't figure out why or what to do about it. You refused to be with me, my pride was stinging, and I think we were both questioning our marriage."

She forgot to breathe. Forgot she *had* to.

"I was hurt at what had become of us. Angry at what you were doing to me." His mouth flattened into a grim line and his eyes half closed, as if he couldn't believe what he was saying. "So I called Chelsea and invited her to dinner."

Lilly felt as if a train was headed for her, but she couldn't move. Couldn't do anything to avoid it.

"I wanted to prove I didn't need you—I didn't love you," he continued hoarsely. "And maybe I wanted to hurt you too. Make you hurt as much as I was hurting."

Lilly pressed her hands to her ears, but he stalked forward and dragged them away.

"I drove her home, I went up to her apartment with every intention of taking her to bed. And then I kissed her and everything felt wrong."

Lilly felt the ground sway beneath her and, cursing, Riccardo scooped her up in his arms. He carried her over to the bench and sat down with her cradled against him. A tortured expression filled his eyes as he stared down at her. "You haunted me. No matter how much you pushed me away you were the only one I wanted."

She sat there in his arms like a strange, disembodied presence that could hear what he was saying but couldn't actually register it. When she managed to speak, her voice was low and thready. "You kissed her but you didn't sleep with her?"

He nodded. "I came home to you and never saw her again."

Something reached inside her and tore her heart out. "What kind of a kiss was it?"

He cursed low under his breath. "You can't torture yourself like that."

"*Yes, I can!*" she shrieked, stumbling off his lap and facing him on shaking legs. "You betrayed me, Riccardo. I saw those photographs. You didn't just kiss her. You had sex with her!"

He frowned. "There were no photographs taken of us. We were in Chelsea's apartment."

"There were *eight*. Eight photos of you in various states of undress. Dammit, stop lying."

He stood up and took her by the shoulders. "You will watch your tongue and tell me what you're talking about."

"Lacey Craig," she threw at him, knowing this might well put the final nail in their marriage, but past caring. "After we got back from Barbados I called her up and asked what proof she had to support her story. She showed me photos of you and Chelsea. *Intimate* photos of you. And she let me buy them to spare me the humiliation of having them splashed across every gossip magazine in the country."

He blinked at her, a look of complete incomprehension on his face. "Let me get this straight," he said slowly. "You called a gossip columnist, demanded information about my infidelity and paid her for fake photos?"

"They weren't fake," she cried. "Everybody in New York knew you were having an affair! Too bad I was the last to know."

His fingers tightened around her shoulders. "They *are* fake photos because I did not sleep with Chelsea Tate— ever—after our relationship began."

His rage and the icy, menacing look on his face vibrated through her like a sledgehammer. Riccardo had never lied to her. Not once in their marriage. Until Chelsea. Truth was like a badge of honor to him—it was the De Campo creed, the way he conducted his life. Better to be brutal and get it over with.

What if she was wrong?

"Lilly?"

She yanked herself out of his grasp and turned away. Her brain moved wildly through the possibilities. Photos could be doctored. They were doctored all the time. Maybe those *hadn't* been shots of him and Chelsea. It had been hard to see their faces after that initial shot of them kissing…

A cold, buzzing feeling descended over her. Would Lacey Craig have dared to sell her fakes? Wouldn't she have been worried Lilly would take them straight to Riccardo, who would have pronounced them as such and sued the hell out of her?

Or maybe Lacey hadn't known they were fake...

Oh, God.

Riccardo took a step toward her, his face hard and determined. "How much did you pay for those photos?"

She shook her head.

"How much?"

"One hundred thousand dollars."

"A hundred thousand?" His brow furrowed. "They wouldn't give you a full-page ad for a hundred grand..."

Lilly felt her world fall apart.

His gaze sharpened on her face as understanding dawned in his eyes. "That was the money you said you sent your parents?"

"Yes."

He sucked in a breath, his fists clenching at his sides. "You trusted me so little you would do that without talking to me?"

"You kissed her, Riccardo! You went home with her, intending to sleep with her. Where in that is there anything that says I should have trusted you?"

His jaw clamped shut. He was silent for several long moments, each one driving the stake that was impaling her heart deeper and deeper.

Finally he raised his gaze to hers and asked quietly, "Was there ever any point in our marriage you were happy?"

She fought the fire burning the back of her eyes. "That first year after we married was the most amazing year of my life. I loved you, Riccardo. I worshipped the ground you walked on. You were my knight in shining armor who'd swooped into my life and made it whole again. But somewhere along the way I lost my glitter when it came to you. You didn't want me the same way you did before. And it was torturous for me to be with you like that." She looked down at the sparkling ring on her finger. "So I left."

"You left because you thought I didn't love you anymore?"

"I left because we were destroying each other. You became obsessed with that job—obsessed with having your birthright. And you left me alone to deal with the fallout of being Lilly De Campo. Something I couldn't do on my own."

He was silent, a granite mask stretching across his face. She hugged her arms around herself and listened as a chorus of tree frogs filled the air with their haunting, rhythmical song.

"You never once thought I might be struggling too? That I might need my wife?" He said the words quietly, deliberately, his face devoid of emotion.

"How would I have known? You're like Mount Vesuvius. You keep everything inside until you explode. And when you do there's nothing for me to respond to but the anger."

His dark gaze rested on her. "I could say the same about you."

"Yes, you could." She nodded. "I have a ton of baggage, I know. But at least I acknowledge mine."

His mouth pulled tight as her arrow hit home. He swung away and walked to the edge of the terrace, rested his elbows on the railing as he looked out at the sea. "I always thought if you wanted something bad enough you made it happen. That we could resolve our differences because we loved each other that much."

The lump in her throat grew so large it felt as if she was aching all over. "Sometimes," she choked, "love isn't enough."

He turned around, his broad shoulders silhouetted against the setting sun. The dull look on his face made the rest of her shrivel away.

"A marriage needs trust to survive. And between the two of us I think we've proved we have none."

And there it was, she thought miserably. Their marriage summed up in one glaring truth.

"It was never going to work."

Her words sat flat and lifeless on the night air between them. Riccardo's head snapped back, a flare of angry color slashing across his cheekbones. His steps as he closed the distance between them were jerky, full of a barely leashed rage that made her suck in a breath. When he stopped in front of her, his furious glare leveled on her face, her heart seemed to stop.

"We may have spoken a lot of truths tonight, Lilly, but do not, *do not* absolve yourself of the responsibility you carry for this marriage. You checked out. You left me. You *chose* to give up. And you *will* own that."

She pulled in another breath, but it wasn't enough, and desperately she dragged in another. There never seemed to be enough oxygen on the planet when she was with Riccardo because he sucked it out of her. Stripped her bare.

He stared at her for a long moment, waiting for her to respond, waiting for her to give him what he demanded of her, but she couldn't force the words out of her mouth.

He spun away and stalked toward the French doors.

"Ric—"

"I need some space."

He disappeared inside. Lilly watched him go, too numb to react. *Where was he going?* The sound of the front door slamming made her heart drop. *He was leaving?*

She ran to the front door and threw it open, but only the glaring darkness of the Caribbean night stared back at her. She would have heard the car if he'd taken it. He must have gone on foot.

She closed the door and fumbled with the deadbolt to lock it. Unsure of what to do next, she turned and leaned against it, pulling in deep, long breaths. Then she slid down to the floor and did the thing she hadn't let herself do since the week she'd left Riccardo.

She sobbed her heart out.

Tears streamed down her face in a barrage that it seemed would never end. Her worst fear about her marriage had been both proven and unproven in one explosive conversation that had left her so raw and exposed she wasn't sure she would ever be able to close herself back up again.

Riccardo had kissed Chelsea Tate with the intent of sleeping with her. And even though he hadn't been able to do it, the fact that he'd kissed Chelsea—the *thought* of him kissing her—splintered Lilly's heart into a million pieces.

How could he? The man who'd promised to love and protect her that day in the cathedral when they'd been married, whom she'd let down all her barriers for, had betrayed her in the worst way possible. Because, she thought numbly, wasn't kissing the most intimate act of all?

Somewhere, someplace deep down inside her, she'd been hoping she was wrong. That Riccardo had been telling her the truth when he'd said nothing had happened between him and Chelsea and that her early naive belief that nothing could touch them was true.

But it wasn't something she could hang onto anymore. She and Riccardo *were* fallible and his message had been clear. *She* had driven him into Chelsea's arms. He had wanted to hurt her as she'd been hurting him. And that, she realized, swiping the tears from her face, was something she'd never thought of. That cool, hard-as-rock Riccardo could be hurt in any way. That *she* had the power to hurt him like that.

But in the end it had been as she'd always known it would be. She hadn't been capable of being what he needed. She hadn't been enough for him. Otherwise he never would have gone to Chelsea.

Her severed heart throbbed with a misery that said there was still some life in it. She closed her eyes and breathed.

To leave had been her survival mechanism. To stop trying to be something she could never be.

But Riccardo's relentless assault continued to unpeel her layers, as if once started it would never stop. Emotions that had been bottled up far too long bubbled over and tumbled into her consciousness. She remembered that perfect day before everything had unraveled, when they'd rescued their dog, Brooklyn, from the street, taken her to the house in Westchester and spent the weekend there. Her gorgeous husband had scooped up Brooklyn in one hand and Lilly in the other and tucked them all into bed. Throwing out the heart-stopping comment as the puppy lay snoring at their feet that maybe they should make theirs a family of four.

She'd been so excited, her mind whirring like the hamster's wheel from her childhood, that she hadn't slept that night. Like the luckiest of little girls on Christmas morning, she'd felt as if she'd been given everything she'd ever dreamed of. She had Riccardo, a great career and a home. A *real* home, where love reigned—not dramatic tension that would take her who knew where next. And for the first time since she'd left Iowa as a teenager, scared and unsure of her future, she'd known everything was going to be okay.

She would have a family of her own—one that wasn't living a hand-to-mouth existence. A family that wasn't a dysfunctional, sordid mess.

Dreams could come true, she'd told herself, falling asleep in Riccardo's arms at dawn.

The impossibly perfect memory made her suck in a breath.

She was still in love with her husband.

No matter how hard she tried to deny it, no matter how much she told herself they shouldn't be together, it was never going to go away. That deep, gnawing pain that had started when she'd left him and never stopped.

She pried her eyes open and stared dully up at the grandfather clock in the hallway. Its rhythmical tick-tock was deafeningly loud in the still villa. She was mad about a man who'd spoken of their love in the past tense tonight. As if he was as sure as she was they'd done too much harm to each other ever to be able to recover from it.

And he was right. About all of it. She *had* shut down on him. She should have told him about her anorexia. She should have told him about the photos. Instead she'd run, like she always did.

But he had kissed Chelsea. And that wasn't something she was sure she could forgive.

She bit her lip, vaguely registering the metallic taste of blood. The clock droned on...tick-tock, tick-tock. She had made huge mistakes in her marriage. But at least tonight she'd taken her first step forward. She'd told the truth. And that was something.

She bit her lip, refusing to give in to the fresh set of tears burning the back of her eyes. If it was clear they were over, then that was for the best. They had closure. In six months she was going to have to walk away from Riccardo, this time for good.

She was going to have to move on.

At least now she could.

She got to her feet, splashed cold water on her face and went back out to the terrace to wait for Riccardo. Two, three hours passed—she wasn't sure. A million stars blanketed the dark Caribbean sky as she drank wine and listened to the rhythmic pull of the ocean.

Her eyes started to drift shut.

The clocks chiming midnight woke her. Disoriented and half asleep, she padded inside to a dark, empty villa. And realized her husband wasn't coming back.

CHAPTER EIGHT

RICCARDO ENDED UP nursing a glass of ten-year-old rum on the front steps of a local rum shack in Holetown. Neat, as the grizzly old proprietor had suggested.

He'd needed a place he could think, away from the glitzy west coast hotels and restaurants. A place where he could digest his mind-blowing conversation with his wife. Because if he'd suspected before that he didn't know all of her it was now brutally apparent he hadn't even scratched the surface of who Lilly De Campo was.

Mind reeling, he'd wandered down the road from the villa until he'd come to the local hotspot—a red-and-cream-painted clapboard house emblazoned with the logo of a local beer company, one of dozens of such dwellings scattered around the island. There had been a handful of Bajans sitting on the front steps, chatting about last night's cricket game, and zero expectations of socializing.

Perfetto.

He took a sip of the rum and was glad the proprietor had talked him into drinking it neat. It brought out the oaky molasses flavor of the blend and right now he needed its smooth burn. Needed to quell the tumult raging through his brain.

His wife had trusted him so little she'd paid a gossip columnist one hundred thousand dollars for pictures that weren't even of him. Then she'd lied to him about where the money had gone.

Che diavolo.

He pulled in a deep breath. What state of mind must she have been in to do something like that? To air their dirty laundry to a tabloid journalist and expose their private lives rather than come to him? He wanted to shake her. To chastise her for being so stupid. Except it had also been his fault. *He* had given her reason to be jealous. *He* had violated the trust in their marriage.

He had almost smeared the past in her face without knowing it by being unfaithful to her like her father had her mother.

He uttered a smothered oath. The bombshells had just kept coming. His wife had been suffering from an eating disorder he hadn't known about. She had been struggling with a disease only made worse by the limelight she'd been thrust into and *he hadn't noticed.* How had he not noticed? It was inconceivable to him. He wasn't an expert on eating disorders, but didn't women usually make themselves throw up when they had one? He knew for sure he hadn't missed that. Lilly hated throwing up, and when she did so because of her migraines she was miserable.

So where had been the signs he'd been supposed to see?

She'd always been tall and thin, and he'd thought that was her natural predisposition, but now that he thought about it she *had* been curvier when they'd met. She'd consistently lost weight throughout their marriage until she'd been ultra-thin at the end, but he'd thought that was because she'd wanted to fit into the designer dresses she'd worn. In hindsight, he admitted, shifting uncomfortably on the steps, her penchant for skipping meals near the end should have raised alarm bells. It was just that he hadn't been home enough to monitor it.

A memory of Lilly, exhausted and seemingly emotionally spent, begging him to let her stay home the night of the financial district's Christmas ball filled his head. He'd thought she was just being difficult and had insisted on her attending because it was a De Campo-sponsored event.

She'd obviously been struggling.

His hands tightened around the glass. He could have destroyed her by not knowing. By continuing to push her. Had he really been that oblivious? Was he so set on perfection in those around him she'd felt she couldn't come to him? Couldn't talk to him?

Had he been, as Lilly had accused, so caught up with his obsession of becoming CEO he hadn't seen anything but the end goal?

An intense feeling of shame washed over him. There had been one month in that last year when he'd only been home one night because he'd been traveling so much, opening restaurants. *One night.*

And maybe there had been more months like that…

"You left me alone to deal with the fallout of being Lilly De Campo."

Was that what he'd done?

He took a swig of the rum and stared out at the cars whizzing by on the snakelike coastal road. Their ability to hurt each other was monumental. The breakdown in communication between them breathtaking. How had something so good gone so wrong?

He watched as a new arrival joined the other grizzled old men on the steps. They clapped him on the back and kept on talking about last night's game, which apparently had been a barn-burner. He was struck by how absolutely insane his life had become. He was a machine, not a man. He no longer remembered what it was like to live because he was too busy planning for tomorrow.

He nursed the glass between his hands and stared down at the brilliant amber liquid. It was time he simplified his life. Step one had been this weekend with Lilly, to discover the truth. Step two would be in three months, when

Antonio ceded control to him. Step three was going to be about honesty.

"I faked my way through our entire marriage."

The statement had made his blood boil. He might have done things all wrong but Lilly had owed him honesty. She had owed that to their marriage. And nothing, *nothing* made up for the fact that she'd walked out on him. And left *him* to deal with the fallout of their marriage.

"It was never going to work."

Her words danced in front of him like a red cape, egging on an enraged bull. If his wife thought she was going to check out again now, when the honesty had just started between them, she was sadly mistaken. Lilly was about to find out what it was like to follow through on a promise. What it was like to pay as he'd been paying for the past year. Because De Campos didn't divorce. They stuck it out—even if they were in a loveless partnership like his parents.

He drained his glass and set it down with a thud that drew the eyes of the faction of grizzled old men. Standing up, he went back inside and slapped his glass on the counter. "Another," he said hoarsely. "Make it a double."

This time he *had left* her.

Lilly stood on the balcony of their villa, staring at the ocean as it sparkled in the moonlight. It was pushing one o'clock and still her husband hadn't come home. He had decided the muddled, mass of confusion his wife undoubtedly was wasn't CEO wife material. Wasn't worth the effort.

Hot, silent tears ran down her cheeks. She'd kept her secrets because she'd known if she'd told the truth about who she was she'd lose him. But in the end it hadn't mattered. She'd lost him anyway.

Had he been repulsed by her secret—by the anorexia that had been her Achilles' Heel? Or had it been the dishonesty? The lies she'd told to save herself?

She didn't blame him for not wanting her. She'd only just started to learn how to appreciate herself.

"I thought you'd be asleep."

Her husband's deep voice came from behind her. She spun around, her heart in her mouth as her gaze moved over his strained, somber features.

"You came back."

"Of course I did." He closed the distance between them. "I told you this is not over between us."

That had been before tonight. Before they had annihilated each other.

His gaze moved over her face. "I've never seen you cry."

She raised a hand to swipe the tears from her face. Telling him she still loved him, that she'd thought she'd lost him forever, wasn't going to happen. Not when she was sure he hated her for what she'd done to him. But she couldn't stop the emotion that was suffocating her, threatening to spill over into something she couldn't control.

His eyes darkened and the strain on his face deepened, looking even harsher in the moonlight. "This is not over," he repeated. "Get that through your head, Lilly. We are only getting started."

How could that be? This reconciliation of theirs was only for six months. And it wasn't real. But tell that to her brain. He did away with the last few inches between them, a look of intent on his face so deliberate her heart stopped in her chest.

"Ric—"

The hand she held out to ward him off was captured and folded against his chest as he pulled her into him. "No more talking," he murmured, moving his lips to the upper curve of her cheek, where the tears were still falling. "We've done enough talking for a lifetime tonight."

She knew she should protest, but then he was kissing away her tears one by one, following the hot, salty path down over the curve of her jaw. As if with every one he dispensed with he was wiping the past away. A sigh was torn from deep inside her as she arched her neck back. If this was supposed to be comfort she couldn't quite envision it, because he was setting her blood on fire.

His big hands swept the straps of her négligée aside so his lips could continue their exploration down the sensitive skin of her neck and over the roundness of her shoulder.

The honesty of this—the honesty of them together like this—had never been in question. And tonight she needed for him to heal them.

To hell with the consequences.

She moved willingly against him as he pulled her up on tiptoes and kissed her—a slow, drugging caress she felt down to her toes. It was like an anesthetic to her soul, his touch, as if the only thing she'd been put on this planet to do was kiss him in these deep, never-ending caresses that devoured the essence of each other.

A shiver ran through her—anticipatory, all-consuming. She buried her fingers in the thick muscles of his shoulders, rediscovering the feel of him under her hands, the way the sharp tug of her teeth on his bottom lip made him groan low in the back of his throat.

"You are killing me," he murmured, sliding his hands down over her silk-covered bottom and yanking her closer.

The feel of his big, warm hands on her, shaping her against the muscular hard length of him made her whimper. His thick erection made her gasp.

"*Esattamente,*" he muttered, scooping her up into his arms. She breathed in the familiar, heady male scent of him as he carried her into the bedroom. It was like coming home.

Light from the big, fat, almost-full moon flooded the beautiful blue-and-white-striped bedroom that looked as if it had come straight out of a magazine. But all Lilly had eyes for was her husband as he let her slide down his body to the floor, the silk catching between them. He was the most smoking hot man she'd ever encountered on so many levels.

Intense, like the night. Exciting, like a summer storm that made everything electric. Earthy, like a man who knew how to savor every moment like the fine wines his family created.

Her heart thumped at the foot of her throat as he slid his fingers under the straps of her négligée and dropped it to the floor. She closed her eyes as his gaze moved over her naked flesh. She had never been perfect but she was definitely less than that now.

"Dio, Lilly. *Come sei bella."*

His raspily intoned observation made her eyes fly open. The look of pure lust on his face made her knees go weak. "I don't look like I used to," she whispered.

He slid his hands down her back to her bottom and tugged her forward, until her naked flesh was flush against his still clothed body. "I told you," he murmured. "I love the curves… If anything, I want you more than I did before."

Oh. Liquid fire raced through her veins as his fingers tangled in the hair at the nape of her neck and he tipped her head back to receive his kiss. Open-mouthed, and hotter than Hades, it immersed her in a pool of want that threatened to eat her alive.

Her control snapped. The depth of her emotion for this man was frightening, endless, but to have him again like this made her frantic, desperate.

"Ric," she muttered against his mouth. "Please."

He abandoned her lips in favor of a fingertips to bare skin exploration of the weight of her breasts. "Do you know how hard it's been for me to keep my hands off you?" he breathed, brushing his thumbs over the tips of her nipples. "I took down a ninety-foot tree in Westchester, I was so crazed."

Lilly squeezed her eyes shut as her nipples hardened beneath his touch. "I can't believe you didn't kill yourself."

"Gabe helped. Matteo got in the way."

She smiled and wriggled against him, trying to get closer, but he closed his hands down hard over her shoulders and held her away.

"Not so fast, *tesoro*. It's been a long time since I've had you like this."

She eased back reluctantly. "Did you really go a year without sex?"

"I'm a man, Lilly. I found ways to ease the tension."

"Oh."

His soft laughter filled the night air. "Don't worry—you were still the star attraction."

The erotic image of him pleasuring himself—stroking that beautiful muscular body of his and thinking about her—sent another hot flash through her body that made her feel vaguely feverish. But then he was kissing his way down her throat toward the sensitive spot at the base of her neck—the spot he knew drove her crazy.

Hot. So hot.

She moved desperately against him.

He slid a hand down over her trembling stomach, over her navel to the juncture of her thighs. "Spread your legs for me, sweetheart."

Lilly swallowed hard and relaxed her grip, letting him push her legs apart.

"Did you ever touch yourself, thinking about me?" he questioned, sliding his fingers against the most private part of her.

"Ric—"

"The truth," he insisted.

"Yes," she murmured. God help her, yes, she had.

He rotated his thumb against the hard, aching center of her. "But it wasn't as good as the real thing, was it? Because I know it wasn't for me."

"No," she groaned. "It wasn't."

He lowered his head and kissed her, made her remember exactly how good he could make her feel. She grabbed a hold of his shirt to steady herself as he slid a finger inside her, his touch so unbearly good she thought she would scream.

"More," she murmured against his lips.

He withdrew and slid two fingers inside her, filling her deeper, harder. She arched against his hand as the ache inside her became unbearable.

"Please," she moaned.

He dropped to his knees in front of her. Lilly made a sound of protest, reaching down and grabbing his arms to pull him back up to her. She felt too exposed, too raw to have him do this to her right now.

But he shook her hands off and looked up at her, eyes glittering. "Immersion therapy, Lilly. Relax and enjoy it."

She squeezed her eyes shut, too hot, too aroused to do anything but obey. And then he was parting her with gentle fingers, his raspy, "*Bella...*" filling the air before he bent and feasted on her. She held the back of his head as he slid his tongue against her aroused flesh. The rush of pleasure that swirled through her was so incredibly good she felt as if every nerve in her body was concentrated right *there*.

"Ric—I need—"

"I know," he murmured against her skin. "Let go, Lilly."

Her legs started to tremble wildly. He slid his fingers inside her again and shot her into another stratosphere. *God.* She just needed him to curve his fingers like—*that.*

"Oh."

He kept his fingers there and flicked his tongue over the hard bud at the center of her. Her insides contracted as she came in a rush of such sweet, hot pleasure he had to hold her upright. It was white-hot, blinding. All-consuming.

She was floating on a sea of pleasure when he got to his feet, scooped her up into his arms and carried her to the bed. "You are so sexy," he murmured, leaning down to kiss her. "Your reactions...everything about you turns me on."

The taste of herself on his lips was unbearably intimate. And she felt her last barrier come tumbling down.

He left her to pull his shirt over his head, his impatient, jerky movements so unlike him she smiled. "Need some help with your pants?"

He stepped closer and brought her hands to his belt.

She took in the hard muscles of his torso, the perfectly defined six-pack, the undeniably hot vee that disappeared beneath his jeans. She had undressed him hundreds of times, but this time her hands were shaking and her throat was dry.

She worked his belt buckle open and fumbled with the button of his jeans.

"Lilly," he murmured, covering her hand with his. "Are you okay?"

She nodded and bit her lip. With a smothered curse he stepped back and shoved his jeans and boxers off. The masculine beauty of his body made her want like a woman who'd been stranded in the desert far too long. When he sank down on the bed and reached for her she straddled his muscular thighs, wanting to give him as much pleasure as he'd given her.

He was hard, aroused, barely leashed male power beneath her, and she wanted him inside her more than she wanted her next breath.

He buried his lips in her shoulder, a tremor running through his big body. "I can't play around like this much longer…"

"Who's playing?" She sat back on her haunches, her eyes riveted to his beautiful toned body. "I'm not," she assured him, sliding her fingers to the insides of his thighs.

His gaze moved to her hands. *Lilly…*

She curved her fingers around him and reveled in his sharp intake of breath. He was smooth and hard like steel, pulsing underneath her fingers. With a muffled curse he sank his hands into her waist and lifted her over him, the movement bringing her swollen flesh into contact with his engorged length.

Ruddy color dusted his cheekbones. "*Maledizione,* Lilly…"

She slid the thick head of him inside her, her body so aroused, so wet, she accommodated him easily. He cursed under his breath, the muscles of his arms bulging as he braced them on either side of himself. She took more of him, and more, until she felt as if she couldn't go further. She'd forgotten how big he was, how the length of him caressed every last centimeter of her. Closing her eyes, she focused on taking him, adjusting her hips until he slid in to the hilt.

Her gasp split the air.

He stayed completely still beneath her while her body adjusted to his, his jaw clenched, his face a picture of grim self-control. "Are you okay?"

"Fine," she breathed, relaxing into him. "You're just so damned big."

He closed his eyes. "That's not usually a complaint."

"It's not, it's j— *Oh, God,* you feel so good."

"*I'd* feel better if I could move," he rasped.

She leaned down and kissed him. "Let me."

She rode him slowly, deliberately at first, every movement designed to drive him wild. He twisted his hips and tried to control the rhythm but she shook her head. "Like this."

He clamped his jaw shut and let her take the lead. Lilly shut her eyes and just *felt.* Felt the size and girth of him stroke her, reach every nerve-ending. Her body clamped around him as she remembered the pleasure he could give her, cried out desperately for it.

No man had ever been able to turn her on this much. Only Riccardo.

She threw her head back and let herself go. Every powerful stroke of his body up into hers was filling her from the inside out—filling the lonely place inside her that had never gotten over the loss of him. And when she looked down at him the dark glitter in his eyes told her he felt it too.

"Are you with me?" he demanded hoarsely. "Please tell me you're with me."

"Always," she whispered.

Something tilted in his face. A look of such raw, uncensored emotion that she felt it in a place she'd never felt it before. He might not love her anymore, but he wasn't devoid of emotion.

She committed it to memory, held onto it as he surged up inside her and demanded she ride him harder, faster. Something told her she was going to need it as he made her drown in the sensations he was creating. As he branded her with his touch and found that sweet spot he knew would take her over the edge. Her fingernails dug into his shoulders as he stroked her deliberately, repeatedly, until she felt the white-hot beginning of her release. Once, twice, three times he drove into her, and she screamed, her body contracting around his in an orgasm stronger and more shattering than the first.

He cursed under his breath and fell back onto his elbows, his body surging up inside her. She felt him throb even bigger, watched his face as he lost control. His hands clamped down on her hips and his body shook in a release that rocked them both.

Winded, shaken to her core, she collapsed forward onto his chest, listening to his heart thunder beneath her ear. This was the time when he'd used to whisper that he loved her in Italian. When he'd tuck her into his side and cradle her until she slept. When she had been sure beyond a shadow of a doubt of his feelings for her.

The hot, humid Caribbean air throbbed around them—heavy and full. A loaded silence stretched between them. They stayed like that for several long minutes. Then Riccardo lifted her off his chest and tucked her beneath the sheets.

"You need to sleep."

She wanted to beg him to hold her. To prolong what they'd shared for just a few more minutes. She heard him snap off the lights and come back to the bed, felt the mattress dipping beneath his weight. Then he reached for her and pulled her into his arms, curving her back against the warm length of him. She exhaled in a long, slow breath. This was enough. Being back in the place where everything felt right. Even for one night.

She fell asleep almost immediately.

Her pounding head woke her at two a.m. She stumbled into the bathroom and grabbed her painkillers out of her bag. She had unscrewed the bottle and downed two tablets with a glass of water when the unthinkable occurred to her.

In the hustle of traveling this morning she'd forgotten to take her birth control pill.

It had been almost twenty-four hours since she had.

"Do me a favor." Alex's words rang in her ear. *"Whatever you do, don't get pregnant."*

She pulled the birth control pills out of her bag and desperately shoved one in her mouth. It hadn't even been twenty-four hours… It would be fine.

But even as she reassured herself she knew it had been stupid, *stupid.* How could she have complicated a relationship in which the only thing that *was* clear was that it didn't need complicating?

CHAPTER NINE

LILLY WOKE UP with such a supreme feeling of well-being she thought she might have been accidentally transported to a land of paradise, where everything was silk sheets, hard male and a bone-meltingly familiar sense of satisfaction she never wanted to end.

Turning her head from its face-down planting in the pillow, she slid her palm across the sheet in search of more warm, hard male. Nothing but silk. Her eyes flickered open. She was alone in the huge king-sized bed.

She flipped over, settled back against the mountain of pillows and stared out at the brilliant blue sky. She might almost think it had been a dream, the ridiculously hot sex she'd had with her husband. But the ache between her legs begged to differ. And in the blinding light of morning everything seemed magnified by ten.

She'd let the man she was still madly in love with, who didn't love her anymore, strip her of the defenses she'd spent a decade building. Then she'd slept with him in a moment of madness without using protection, which demonstrated exactly what a moment of madness it had been.

Damn.

She squeezed her eyes shut. It had been a monumentally stupid thing to do. The one thing she'd never been able to deny was the connection they'd had in bed. And once that took over all bets were off.

It was the reason she'd refused to see him for so long. Because she didn't trust herself around Riccardo.

Her stomach churned. Both she and Riccardo had extremely fertile families. But hadn't it taken her girlfriend, Darya, forever to conceive? Surely it wouldn't happen in one night?

Finding the whole thing entirely too disconcerting, she threw back the covers and swung her legs out of bed. Riccardo would have been up hours ago. He'd probably swum fifty lengths of that Olympic-sized pool and gone through every set of weights in the exercise room by now.

She padded restlessly over to the patio doors and threw open the curtains. The humid heat hit her immediately, and the perfume-soaked, salty, heavy air was filled with the scent of dozens of exotic flowers. It begged complete lethargy—a sunchair, a book and a drink, followed by a cool swim.

She blinked and shaded her eyes against the brilliant sunlight. And found her guess had been right. But rather than laps her husband was slicing through the ocean with a powerful front crawl that ate up the distance between the raft that bobbed about a mile out and the beach.

She watched as he hit the shore and walked up the beach, water sluicing down over his washboard abs. The drool that formed in her mouth was swift and uncontrollable. As if having him so completely last night had done nothing to stem the urge she had for him.

He lifted a hand to swipe the water from his face. And saw her standing there.

A heart-meltingly sexy smile curved his mouth. He walked up the beach and came to stand below the balcony, a fully relaxed, content-looking Riccardo who turned her insides to mush.

"You coming down?"

A smile twisted her lips. "If you'll come swimming with me. I'm sweating already."

"We have fifteen minutes before breakfast is ready. Get your suit on and get down here."

She slipped off her négligée and pulled on the fuchsia bikini she'd bought with Alex. She might have made the huge mistake of sleeping with Riccardo last night, but that didn't mean she had to continue her foolish behavior today. She needed to focus on keeping her head. She bit her lip as she pulled on a short cotton dress over her bathing suit. So what was she doing, running down to swim with him? And what had he meant when he'd said, *"This is not over. We are only getting started"?*

It didn't matter what he'd said! She swiped some sunscreen across her cheeks and nose. Riccardo *was* a lethal banned substance for her. Best to accept that last night had been inevitable between them, like a storm reaching its conclusion, and find a way to make it through the next six months without killing each other.

Hot sex wasn't going to accomplish that.

A rational brain would.

Tell that to her hormones, she thought as she joined Riccardo on the tiny private beach in front of the villa, the sand as smooth as silk between her toes. Because the intensity of her husband's dark gaze on her was making her overheating problem a virtual crisis.

"You'd better lose the dress," he advised. "Nowhere down here to leave it."

She darted a self-conscious glance around her. The bikini wasn't French Riviera material but it was revealing enough. She would rather have just gotten in the water, but since there really wasn't anywhere to leave her cover-up on the beach she walked up to the terrace, draped it over a chair and headed back down to him, self-conscious in her halter top bikini.

The smell of bacon wafted through the air. "Mrs. Adams is cooking?"

He nodded. "We thought we'd let you sleep in. You needed it."

She walked toward him, ultra self-conscious in her halter top bikini.

Her husband took her in from beneath veiled lashes. "And here I thought we had declared a truce."

She frowned. Looked down at herself. *Pink.* Her swimsuit was pink.

Heat filled her cheeks. "It was the only suit that didn't make me look like an adult movie star."

He reached for her, his fingers closing over her forearm. "Why go for modest when you look that good, *cara?*"

She sucked in a breath as he pulled her against his hard, dripping wet body. "Did you listen to a word I said last night?"

"*Si.* I am intent on desensitizing you."

She pressed a hand against his chest to balance herself. "You can't just wave your fairy wand and cure me, Riccardo. Anorexia is something I'll carry with me for the rest of my life, even if I have it under control."

"I know," he said, bringing his lips down on hers as he swung her up in his arms. "But I'm going to do it anyway."

She smiled at his arrogance. His lips were warm from the heat of the sun, his kiss as leisurely as the mood he seemed to be in, and she found she just didn't have the willpower to fight him.

He walked into the sea, and the water was so warm it barely registered on her heated skin. Then he wrapped her legs around him so they floated on the buoyant sea.

"Riccardo…"

"What?"

"I—I don't think this is appropriate."

He gave her an amused look. "We're married. What's inappropriate about it?"

She focused her gaze on his Adam's apple. "Last night

was…amazing…but I think anymore of that is just going to complicate things between us."

He lifted her chin with his fingers. "If you mean sex, Lilly, then I'm going to have to disagree. Sex breaks down the barriers between us, and if you think, now that we're finally talking, I'm going to let you put them up again, you're mistaken. By the end of this weekend there isn't going to be anything I don't know about you."

She went rigid. "There isn't anymore to say."

He pressed his lips together. "How did you keep it from me? I never saw the signs."

"My anorexia?"

He nodded.

She pressed her hands against his chest to put some distance between them, but he kept his arms firmly banded around her. "I was better when I met you. I'd gotten control over it. I'd spent my career practicing physiotherapy, learning how incredible the human body is—how strong it is—and how much more important it was to honor your body than do what I'd been doing to it."

She swallowed hard. His gaze on her face was making her feel as if she was under a microscope.

"It started to get bad for me again after that first year, when our honeymoon with the media wore off and they made a game out of criticizing how I looked or what I wore."

"Which they do with anyone who's in the limelight like that," he interjected.

"Yes. But for me it was harder. Anorexia isn't something with a lot of outward signs. It's insidious. I withdraw. I stop eating. It becomes impossible for me to look at my body objectively. Everything gets distorted."

He frowned. "I thought it was a vanity thing. The need to look perfect."

A rueful smile curved her mouth. "The need to not hate myself would be more accurate."

His jaw hardened. "Was I really that impossible to talk to? Did I really demand that much perfection from you?"

"It comes with your life, Riccardo. It's *expected* from those around you."

His jaw hardened. "We could have made adjustments to our life to make things easier for you."

She shook her head. "You're going to be the head of a ten-billion-dollar conglomerate when you take over from your father. You couldn't make those changes even if you wanted to."

His dark eyes glittered. "We could have. We could have done what was necessary and let the rest go."

"You're a dreamer," she bit out. "You needed a new wife. And you refused to admit it."

His lip curled. "I did not need a new wife. I needed a wife with the guts to tell me what was wrong. I needed a wife who was there for me at one of the lowest points of my life and instead you were *gone*."

She recoiled. "I had lost myself, Riccardo. I had lost the ability to keep myself in balance. If I hadn't left I would have reverted back to my old bad habits and destroyed myself."

A muscle jumped in his jaw. "You couldn't have waited until I'd gotten back? Been there for me?"

She pushed hard against his chest and this time he let her go. Finding the sandy bottom with her feet, she stood facing him. "What happened in Italy? All I knew was that you'd been summoned there on Antonio's orders."

He scraped his wet hair out of his face. "It doesn't matter now. We're talking about why you left."

"Goddammit, Riccardo." She took a step closer and jabbed her finger in his face. "We *are* talking about why I left. You never talk. You never tell me how you're feeling. What the hell happened in Tuscany?"

His face tightened into a stony stillness. "I knew the restaurant business was the future for De Campo. Knew we needed to diversify. Antonio didn't agree. He forbade me to proceed with the plans I had for Orvietto." He paused. "I signed the lease anyway."

She let out a slow breath. "He lost his mind…?"

"He threatened to strip me of my title and kick me out of the company."

"What?" Her mouth dropped open. "He wouldn't have done that."

"He would have!"

She took a step back as he practically yelled the words at her.

"The only reason he didn't was because my decision was right. I *proved* him wrong. Orvietto proved him wrong. But when I came back to New York that night I thought I'd lost everything. I'd given up the sport I loved for an old man who didn't give a damn, I was about to lose my job at De Campo, and then I walked into our house—into our *empty* house—to find the only person who could make me feel better and a teary Magda informed me you'd gone. *Gone.*" His gaze, dark and tormented, swept over her. "I hadn't slept in forty-eight hours. I just looked at her and said, 'Gone? What do you mean, gone?'"

Lilly felt a wave of nausea sweep over her. She'd been so lost in her own private hell she'd been numbed against the bizarre, disjointed tone of his voice when he'd called that night from overseas.

"I'm sorry," she whispered, tears stinging the back of her eyes. "I'm so sorry."

He looked away, the sun reflecting off the hard line of his jaw. "It isn't always about you, Lilly."

She wrapped her arms around herself. "I never thought it was."

The waves lapped gently around them, the only sound in this private slice of paradise.

"How did things ever get so bad between you two?"

He looked back at her. "Between Antonio and I?"

She nodded.

"The day of my graduation from Harvard I told him I'd signed with TeamXT. It was a once-in-a-lifetime opportunity I couldn't say no to. I'd been driving every summer, whenever I could, but this—this was my chance. I told Antonio I needed a couple of years to get it out of my system—that I'd join De Campo after that." He shrugged. "I knew he wasn't going to be happy, but I thought, given the opportunity, he might understand." A bitter note filled his tone as he continued. "I should have known better. He gave me an ultimatum instead. Join De Campo or forget ever being a part of it."

"You walked away?"

"We didn't speak after that until he became ill and asked me to take over."

"He expected you to come back after all that?"

He exhaled roughly. "You have to understand Antonio's background. His father was a tyrant. He browbeat Antonio into running the business when all my father ever wanted to do was work with animals. He wanted to raise prize-winning racehorses, not prize-winning vines, but his father had built a thriving business and Antonio was expected to take over."

"So by following your dream with racing you became everything he'd ever wanted to be?"

"*Sì.* I was the ultimate insult."

"So why not choose Gabe to head the company? He has such a love for it."

He grimaced. "Antonio is old-fashioned. He could never get past the fact that his eldest son should carry on as CEO. And, despite the animosity between us, we have always been the same. Tough sons-of-bitches who know how to get what we want."

How true *that* was. She blinked, trying to absorb it all. "And what about your mother? She didn't interject through all of this?"

"You've met her," he said roughly. "My mother toes the party line. Their marriage is based on mutual ambition. Emotion doesn't have anything to do with it. Not with her boys, either. She would have carted us off to boarding school in true aristocratic fashion if my father hadn't insisted we learn the wine business."

Emotions swirled inside her. Suddenly she wasn't certain of anything anymore. Whether she'd been right to leave him. Whether she should have worked harder at her marriage. It was all riddled with intricacies she had no way of assimilating.

"So what now?" she asked huskily. "You wait while Antonio strings you along?"

He shook his head. "He's retiring in three months. He's promised to hand De Campo over to me then. *If*," he murmured bitterly, "I continue to prove to him I deserve it."

She flinched. "You could walk away. Go back to racing…"

His expression turned black as night. "I can't go back."

"You can do anything you want. You're a winner, Riccardo. You move mountains when you need to."

"You think I don't want to?" The words exploded out of him. "Every morning when I was driving I woke up feeling lucky to be on this planet. I was free. I was *alive*. Everytime I stepped on that racetrack I challenged the very core of myself. I was the *best*. The adrenalin, that charge that came at the starting line from driving a vehicle more powerful than any other on the planet—it *defined* me."

"So do it," she urged. "You don't owe Antonio anything. This is your life, not his."

His broad shoulders stiffened. "This is about honor. Not about doing what I want. Something I'm not sure *you* know much about. You walked away from your family and you walked away from me. But sometimes you have to hang in there, Lilly. Sometimes you have to fulfill the promises you've made. Even if it interferes with the grand plan."

His anger rippled through her, the depth and fury of it rocking her back on her heels. It was too much. Too much had passed between them. There was no going back.

"I think we should get some breakfast," she murmured, needing to break the intensity. "Mrs. Adams must have it ready by now."

"By all means." He nodded savagely. "Wouldn't want the eggs to cool while you do a little soul-searching."

She turned her back on him and started walking. Five and a half months. She could do this.

If it was possible to spend the day in heaven and feel as if you were in hell, then Lilly had managed to capture perfectly that peculiar and miserable experience. She'd spent the day on the private beach with an introspective version of her husband, surrounded by a shimmering sexual tension that was impossible to ignore despite the fact it seemed they were a million miles apart.

Somehow guilt had taken center stage. She should have been there for Riccardo when he'd been struggling. His account of coming home to find her gone had torn her heart out. No matter what she'd been going through, she should have been there for him.

She'd been incredibly selfish. Not only with her marriage. With her life. She'd had a dream for herself. To leave Mason Hill and never look back. But in pursuing that dream she'd hurt a lot of people. Her parents, Lisbeth—who'd been left alone and defenseless, even if she *had* been too young to come with them—and her brother, who'd been left with her and Alex's work on the farm. And, although she would do the same thing over, she'd had to leave to be who she was now, she was starting to realize that by being so wrapped up in herself she'd neglected the people she loved.

Her heart gave a painful squeeze. Even now she was

here and not with Lisbeth, helping her through her treatment.

When she got better, Lilly was going to bring her to New York to stay with her. She was going to make up for leaving her alone in Iowa.

"What are you thinking about?"

Riccardo's idly delivered question was one of the few he'd uttered over their evening meal at the beachfront restaurant on Barbados's south coast. It pulled her out of her thoughts and focused her attention on the man sitting across from her. Not that she'd been able to avoid acknowledging how good he looked. Dressed in jeans and a gray T-shirt, he had a relaxed and dangerously attractive air about him that every woman in the restaurant had already noticed. Including the Hollywood A-lister and the Mediterranean Princess sitting at right angles to them.

He hadn't looked at one of them.

"So?" He lifted his hand and waved it at her.

She took a sip of her wine—just because Riccardo had refused alcohol tonight it didn't mean she had to. "Is this going to be your new occupation? Analyzing me at every moment?"

His gaze narrowed. "Until I'm sure you're telling the truth—*si,* it is."

She waggled her fingers at him. "No secrets left here. I'm an open book."

Except I still love you desperately.

"You're thinking about something."

About how she'd like to skip dessert, rush home and enjoy that incredible body of his as the final course... Which was absolutely, positively not going to happen.

His mouth tilted up at the corners. "You know the rules. You look at me like that—we leave." He reached into his jeans pocket and threw his wallet on the table.

She stared at the wallet, her heart pounding. "I wasn't

looking at you like that. And we should at least look at the dessert menu."

"Why? You never eat dessert." He handed his credit card to the waiter. "Tell me what happened to your wedding rings."

She set her glass down with a jerky movement. "I told you I'm not sure where they are."

He lifted a brow. "I may be a lot of things, *tesoro,* but I'm not a fool. You're far too careful with things to lose them. So where are they?"

Her gaze slid away from his. "I'm not sure you want to know."

He lifted his brow higher.

"They might be in the East River."

"Scusi?"

She swallowed hard. "I threw them off the Brooklyn Bridge."

His jaw dropped. "You threw your fifty-thousand-dollar engagement ring off the Brooklyn Bridge?"

"I was angry."

"You were *angry?*" For the first time in their married life her husband looked speechless.

She lifted her chin. "The day I left I was so mad, so hurt. I had a clinic in Brooklyn and on my way back I lost it. I felt so betrayed—about Chelsea, about what you'd done to us—that I asked my cab driver to stop and I just…"

"Threw them in," he finished grimly.

"Sure I can't get you anything else?" Their waiter popped a leather folder on their table.

"I wanted to have a liqueur." Lilly searched desperately for anything that wouldn't involve them being alone together.

"We can have one at the villa."

"I'd prefer to have it here." She looked desperately at the little bar that sat beside this restaurant on the beach. There was loud Calypso music playing and lots of locals hanging out on the front patio. "Why don't we have one *there?* It looks like fun."

He followed her gaze. "Trying to avoid the inevitable, Lil?"

"I'm trying to have a good time. You might try that every once in a while."

The antagonism that flared in his gaze made her stomach do a little flip. He threw some money on the table and stood up.

"One drink."

Breathing deeply at her momentary reprieve, Lilly settled herself on a stool at the beachside bar and smiled at the tall, dreadlocked Bajan bartender.

He eyed them up. "On your honeymoon?"

Lilly choked.

"I wish we were," Riccardo interjected drily. "The *signora* would like a drink."

Mr. Dreadlocks, whose hair reached further down his back than her own, shifted his oh-so-cool gaze to her. "What can I get you?"

"How about the house specialty?"

He blinked. "The house specialty?"

"Sure. Sounds good."

"Lewis," he introduced himself, sticking a hand out. She took it, then he did the same to Riccardo. "The same?"

"Wouldn't miss it. But make mine a half—I'm driving."

Lewis pulled about five different bottles off the shelf and started mixing. Lilly could tell she'd made a big mistake by the time he got to bottle number three, which had no label on it and looked as if it was a home brew.

Riccardo held his glass up to hers, a challenging glitter in his ebony eyes. "Bottoms up."

It was so strong it was all Lilly could do not to plug her nose and drink it that way. Those who liked straight alcohol might have found it passable, and Riccardo wasn't having any trouble with it, but for Lilly, who wasn't used to drinking liquor neat, every sip felt like a fire in her mouth and throat.

Every sip was also making her feel looser and much less inhibited. She permitted herself a good look at her drool-worthy husband. Imagined stripping off that T-shirt and exploring every inch of his hard pecs and chest. *Would allowing herself one more night be such a huge mistake?* After all, it wasn't as if this was easy, being here in such a romantic place. Maybe after this weekend, back in New York, she'd be able to keep a much firmer grip on her head.

Determinedly she rattled on to Lewis about how much she loved the island and asked him a million questions about himself.

Riccardo drained his glass and set it on the bar. "Time to go."

She scrunched her face up and downed the rest of her drink. She was going to need it. She was definitely going to need it. Lewis waved goodnight and made them promise to come back.

Their walk to the car was filled with a weighty silence that played on Lilly's nerve-endings like a bow. Her whole body felt as if it was on fire.

"What the hell was in that drink?" she muttered, leaning against the car while Riccardo opened her door.

He whipped the door open, then pushed her back against the Lamborghini. "I'm not sure I want to know."

Her fingers curled into his shirt as he leaned down and took her mouth in a hard, punishing kiss that told her he was still furious about the rings. But it was the heat behind it that made her feel light-headed.

This was going to be off the scale.

Riccardo considered himself a skilled driver, but there was no finesse in the way he handled Charles Browne's sleek sports car as they drove the windy coastal road home. Lilly was all over him. It was all he could do to keep the car on the road with her unbuttoning his shirt and sliding her hands over his chest.

"Lilly," he groaned. "What are you doing?"

"What's the matter, Mr. Racecar Driver?" she taunted, sliding her hands to his belt. "A little distraction and you can't cope?"

He sucked in a breath as she tugged hard on the leather. "I never should have let you have that drink."

"So true," she murmured. The rasp of his zipper was agonizingly loud in the quiet confines of the car. "Too late now."

Her fingers brushed over him. He jerked so hard the car went sliding across the road. He shoved her away from him and yanked hard on the wheel to avoid a ditch. "If you want to live, keep your hands off me."

She slunk back against the seat. He glanced at her impatient expression. *Dio.* What had gotten into his wife? He hadn't seen this Lilly since—when? He couldn't remember.

His body throbbing with an urgency that was near combustible, he started inwardly reciting the specs of the engine under the Lamborghini's hood. One after another he went through the parts, until he'd exhausted every single screw and cap and they were on the side road to the villa.

He brought the car to a growling halt in the garage, walked around to Lilly's side and pulled her out. "You're paying for that," he promised, pushing her in front of him and out of the garage. "That was seriously stupid, Lilly."

His wife appeared not to care. In fact she stood there, her cat's eyes challenging him, focused on him, as he unlocked the door to the villa. He urged her inside and locked it. The want in her gaze undid him.

He threw her over his shoulder and headed upstairs.

"You know I like this," she teased.

"Your payment hasn't even begun."

He set her down on the floor of their bedroom, then shrugged out of his shirt, ripped off his belt and ditched his pants. Lilly's eyes were big as saucers as he pushed her against the wall and ran his hand over the soft flesh of her breasts, temptingly full under her cotton dress, then down over her trembling stomach.

"Ric—"

He moved his hands over her hips and under the flirty dress that had been driving him crazy all night. Her flesh was warm, and toned, and control was in short supply.

"Feel free to tell me when the punishment is over."

He pushed her thighs apart and slid the heel of his hand up over the heat of her. "You will know."

She was trembling under his hands. He reached up, snagged his fingers in the sides of her barely-there thong and pulled it down over her long legs. She was beautiful and intoxicating, his Lilly, and she whispered something unintelligible as he stood and buried his fingers in her hair, kissing her senseless. She had the most perfect lips he'd ever encountered in a woman—full, perfectly shaped, and without a collagen injection in sight. And if he hadn't been so intent on teaching her a lesson he would have suggested she wrap them around another part of his anatomy.

But payback was paramount. He slid a hand between her thighs, seeking and finding her hot wetness. She moaned and pressed closer, inviting him in as he slid a finger inside her.

"Ric—"she said brokenly, shaking like a leaf.

"Not over," he said harshly, adding another finger and working her in a rhythm he knew would send her close to the edge.

Her breathing was quick and tortured against his mouth. Her hips writhed against his hand. And he knew the point at which she would beg…

"Please—I—"

He removed his fingers from her and pushed her toward the bed. "I never make a promise I don't keep, *amore mio.*"

The front of her knees butted up against the edge of the

mattress. He placed a palm in the small of her back and pushed her forward until her hands were braced on the bed.

"Almost over," he murmured. "Because I know you like it like this too."

She bit back a gasp as he pushed her dress up and nudged her legs apart.

"Ric—"

"Shh." He leaned over and pressed a kiss against her back. "Keep your hands there and don't move."

She stayed where she was. He felt his composure waver as he brushed himself against the wet heat of her, hard steel against soft velvet. Lilly groaned and grasped the bedcovers. She was as hot for him as he was for her, but he kept a torturous hold on himself as he slid into her slowly, inch by inch. She was incredibly vulnerable in this position and he needed her trust.

"Good?" he asked hoarsely, giving her body a chance to adjust to the size and girth of him.

She let out a strangled, urgent moan. He closed his eyes and let himself go. Let the desperate urgency of a man who was haunted by a woman take over as he drove into the tight, wet heat that embraced him like a glove.

Too long he had wanted her. Too much he had missed her.

His hands tightened on her hips as he took her close to the edge, then pulled back, wanting this to last, wanting to torture her as she'd tortured him. Wanting to give them both maximum pleasure. But his body tensed and swelled; his mind fixed on the torturously perfect fit of being inside of her again. Then the world splintered apart.

He wanted, *needed* her to be there with him, and he almost cried out with relief when he felt her body contract around his, drawing out his own release until his harsh moan split the night air. The tightening of her body rolled over him like a shockwave, sending surge after surge of explosive pleasure through him.

Dio. He scooped her trembling body off the bed and sat down with her limbs wrapped around him. She buried her head in his shoulder as if she couldn't bear to break the connection. And the force of his emotion hit him like a tidal wave, stealing his breath.

He was not over her. He was not even close to being over her.

She had walked out on him without a backward glance. He had spent every night after that for at least a month thinking she would change her mind and come home.

She hadn't.

He stood up with an abrupt movement and deposited Lilly on the bed. She stared up at him, a dazed look on her face, all tangled long limbs and physical satiation.

Great sex, he told himself. *That's all it is.* But it was enough to severely mess a man's head up.

"I'm going to go make sure everything's locked up," he said roughly.

She was curled in a ball on her side of the bed when he came back. A tightness seized his belly so strong he almost reached down to gather her in his arms. But he kept his hands clenched tightly by his sides.

She deserved to suffer.

He'd suffered every night for a year. Let her feel his pain.

CHAPTER TEN

LILLY PEEKED HER head around her sister Lisbeth's hospital room door, checking to see if she was awake. Their brother David, who'd driven Lisbeth down to New York last night for a series of tests before her treatment abroad, was sitting in a chair by the window.

"Lilly!" Lisbeth practically screamed the word across the room at her, her blue eyes shining brightly. "You're here!"

Lilly crossed the room, gave her older brother a hug, then pressed a kiss to her sister's cheek. Lisbeth had an IV tube sticking out of her arm and looked so pale and small that a lump formed in her throat. This had to work. There was no alternative.

"Where is Riccardo? Did you bring him?"

Lilly shook her head and sat back. She needed to tell Riccardo about Lisbeth, and soon, because she and Alex intended on going to Switzerland with her. But it never seemed like the right time—not with the rollercoaster of emotion going on between them. "I will soon, sweetie. How are you feeling?"

Her sister made a face. "Crappy, but the doctor's hoping after all this I'm going to feel a whole lot better."

Lilly's heart contracted, feeling too big for her chest. "Six weeks, Lizzie. You can do it."

"Does you and Riccardo being back together mean I can

come stay with you guys when I'm better?" Lisbeth looked at her with eager eyes.

Lilly kept her face straight, because to do anything else would be to reveal far too much to her sister and brother about her and Riccardo's relationship. "You can come stay with us anytime."

You can come stay with me *anytime.*

A satisfied smile curved her sister's lips. "I think I need a life."

Lilly squeezed her hand. "Conserve your energy so we can fight this battle together. Then we'll talk about it."

They stayed until Lisbeth got tired and David had to leave for home. Kissing their sister goodbye, they walked out into the hallway.

"She's going to be okay, right?" Lilly asked, looking up at her older brother.

David pulled her into a hug. "Of course she is."

She hugged him tight, her head feeling far, far too full. She loved her serious, hardworking sibling, even with his strict sense of right and wrong—which had clearly labeled her and Alex's defection nine years ago *wrong.* Seeing him again after so long—what had it been? A year and a half? Two years—reminded her how much she missed him.

Her brother pulled back. "You okay? You look like hell, sis."

No. She most definitely was not okay. But she couldn't talk to David about it.

"I'm fine. Just worried."

"Pretty damn amazing we can get her this treatment. She'll be fine, Lil. We didn't raise her to be a strong, sturdy farmgirl for nothing."

She nodded. "You sure you want to head back tonight? You could stay and start out early tomorrow. A few hours isn't going to make a difference."

"It will the way things are now." Her brother rubbed a hand against his face. "Even with the extra money you've been sending and the extra help we've hired we've all been working from sun-up till sun-down."

Guilt mixed with the maelstrom of emotion swirling through her. She felt as if she was hanging on by a thread. "I'm sorry," she whispered. "You know we had to go."

The lines of fatigue softened around the corners of his mouth. "I know. In some ways I think Mom and Dad even understand too. But staying away isn't going to change the past. It's only driving the wedge deeper and deeper between you guys."

"I know." And she knew she had to do something about it. "Are things any better between them?"

"Not unless you count the fact they've given up fighting with each other." He lifted his shoulders. "I think they're just numb to it all now."

She wasn't sure if that was a good or bad thing. "I was thinking of coming home for Mom's birthday."

"She would love that. She misses you, Lilly. She doesn't say anything—you know Mom—but she does."

A lump formed in her throat. "About Lisbeth…"

He shook his head. "She needs to get out. We can't keep her where she doesn't want to be."

"But the farm…"

"We'll manage. The extra money is helping a lot."

At least something good was coming out of a reconciliation that only seemed to get more complicated with every day that passed.

Speaking of which… She glanced at her watch. "I need to go. I'm late for dinner with Riccardo."

She hugged her brother, watched as he headed in the direction of the parking garage and then pushed through the front doors of Memorial Sloan Kettering. Flagging a cab, she slid in and gave the driver directions to the restaurant where she was to meet Riccardo.

She rested her head against the seat and closed her eyes. It had been seven weeks since her and Riccardo's weekend in Barbados. Seven weeks during which she'd been telling herself she could walk out when their deal was done. Then she'd walked into her doctor's office this morning to confirm what she'd been desperate to deny.

She was pregnant. Exactly seven weeks pregnant. With her soon-to-be ex-husband's baby.

If she'd consciously set out to create a bigger disaster, she couldn't have done so.

How was a baby going to fit into all this?

She stared numbly out at the rush-hour Manhattan traffic, bumper to bumper, horns blaring. She'd spent the past seven weeks trying to blend her and Riccardo's lives in a way that eased confrontation. She'd done the things she had to do for her practice, refused to give up the friends and essential things that had made her life her own over the past year—*and* fulfilled her commitments as Riccardo's wife. Surprisingly, it had worked rather well.

Riccardo seemed bent on reducing the stress placed on her, and had instructed Paige to accept only the social invitations that were essential to De Campo's interests. He was like a guard dog, monitoring her with annoying persistence. And it made her wonder if there would have been a different outcome for them if it had been like this all along.

Pain stabbed at her insides. The ache inside her was deep and all-consuming. She'd been trying so hard to ignore her feelings for him—to keep herself intact. But every time she tried to put distance between them Riccardo would knock the walls down. He came home early, insisted they eat together, and this time around they actually talked. About which way the board was leaning toward a CEO. How delayed tiles meant Zambia would open a week late. About Antonio being a piece of work.

And then there were the nights… He had followed through on his promise that there would be sexual intimacy. And it was the one thing she couldn't deny him. Or herself.

It was becoming harder and harder to remind herself that

this was a business arrangement when in so many ways
this was the marriage she'd never had.

The cab swung to a halt in front of Toujours, a new,
eclectic French bistro in the financial district which Riccardo was courting to stock De Campo's new Napa Valley
vintages. She had met the owner, Henri Thibout, formerly
a chef in Paris, at a party a few weeks before, and knew
Toujours was at the top of her husband's expansion list.

Henri stood as the maître d' ushered her to the table.
Lilly's eyes widened when she saw the tall man standing
behind him. *Antonio.* What was he doing here? Riccardo
hadn't mentioned anything about him being in town.

"Lilly." Henri, a short, balding man in his mid-fifties,
who made up for it with bucketloads of charm, brushed
twin kisses to her cheeks and introduced her to his head
sommelier, Georges, and his wife Joanna.

Riccardo stood and brushed a similar kiss to both her
cheeks. She felt the tension radiating from him. *Great,* she
thought, turning to Antonio. Exactly what she needed tonight. The battle of the De Campos.

The big, burly, aristocratic man, with his hook nose
and formidable features, failed to intimidate her tonight.

Maybe because she was *pregnant.* If she said it ten more
times maybe she'd believe it.

Henri reached for the sparkling wine chilling on the
table and pulled Lilly's glass toward him. "This will do
the trick after a long day," he said jovially. "Riccardo says
you work long days."

"None for me, thank you," Lilly said quickly. "It *has*
been a long day. I might actually fall flat on my face if I
do."

Riccardo shot her a quizzical look. If there was anything
Lilly loved it was a good sparkling wine. She averted her
gaze and answered Joanna's question about what she did
for a living.

The five-course tasting menu was superb, but the smell

of seafood was making her nauseous. She did her best, but by the time she'd forced herself to eat half of her third course chicken dish she thought she was going to choke. She set her fork and knife down in an abrupt movement that sent the clang of fine china echoing throughout the restaurant.

Conversation stopped. "Is it not to your liking?" Henri enquired, frowning. "I can get you some—"

"It's delicious," Lilly assured him. She reached for her water. "Apologies—my appetite is a bit off."

Riccardo kept that watchdog look on her, his gaze darkening. She stumbled through the sorbet and cheese course, so desperate to be home alone with her thoughts that she almost jumped out of her seat at the end of the meal.

"Thank you," she murmured to Henri after he'd promised Riccardo feedback on the wine list by next week. "It was lovely to see you again."

Antonio stayed behind to enjoy an aperitif with Henri. She watched her husband's mouth tighten at the interaction. Antonio was in town without Francesca, as usual, who preferred not to travel to North America. He and Henri had obviously hit it off.

Riccardo led her through the restaurant, his firm grip on her elbow keeping her by his side. When they'd stepped out of the busy restaurant onto the sidewalk he spun her around.

"What is up with you? *Dio.* It's like you've had a gallon of coffee in one go."

She pulled her arm out of his. There was *no way* she was telling him her news on a busy Manhattan sidewalk.

"Like I said. It's been a long day. What was Antonio doing here?"

"Sticking his nose where it doesn't belong, as usual," he growled. "Don't deflect, Lilly. You were a disaster in there. You hardly ate a thing. In fact you've hardly eaten a thing for weeks. This is ending *now.*"

She focused her gaze a centimeter to the right of his. "I'm feeling a bit nauseous, that's all."

"Then we're going to see your doctor," he said grimly. "I will not have you go through this again."

"I did see my doctor. I'm fine."

"Then what's wrong?" He stalked closer and captured her wrist in his. "We are not moving until you tell me."

"I think we should—"

"Lilly!" The valet who had been headed toward them stopped in mid-stride as Riccardo bellowed the word at her. "Spit it out."

His anger, her terror, and the complete loss of control she was feeling all hit her at once. "I'm pregnant!" she yelled at him. "I'm pregnant, goddammit, Riccardo. There—are you happy?"

He went chalk-white under his olive skin. The valet swiftly changed direction. The two of them faced off like prize fighters on the busy sidewalk. Then Riccardo grabbed her arm and pulled her under the awning of the restaurant, away from the flow of people.

"Is it mine?"

Her jaw dropped open. "I can't believe you're asking me that."

"It could be Taylor's."

She put a hand on her stomach. "I'm seven weeks pregnant. *Exactly* seven weeks pregnant. It's yours."

He went even paler, raking a hand through his hair. "We're not having this conversation here."

"I was trying to avoid it," she muttered. "And I sincerely hope that valet doesn't realize what a scoop he has on his hands."

Riccardo walked over to the valet stand and said something to the young guy, who practically ran to the lot across the street. He came back minutes later with the Jag.

Riccardo opened the door. "Get in."

They didn't talk for the entire drive home. Her husband's

knuckles were white on the steering wheel, his attention focused on the road. When they got to the house he opened the door, slammed it behind her and directed her inside.

She flicked on the lights in the front sitting room and sat down on the sofa. Riccardo poured himself a Scotch and paced the room like a restless, lethal animal that had no idea what its next move would be.

Finally he stopped by the fireplace and rested an elbow on the mantel, his gaze sinking into her. "It happened in Barbados if that's the timing."

She nodded. "I forgot my pill that morning we flew down. I didn't realize it until after we'd had sex."

His gaze narrowed. "You didn't see fit to tell me?"

She pressed her lips together. "The chances of anything coming from it were minuscule."

"Well, it happened," he growled. "You should have told me."

She got to her feet, feeling too vulnerable while he towered over her. "What difference would it have made? It happened. Now we're going to have to decide how we're going to deal with it."

He was in front of her so fast her head spun, his fingers biting into her arms. "We are *having* this baby."

"Of course we are." She stared at him, aghast. "Well, technically *I* am having this baby, and *we* are going to have to figure out how it'll work after we separate."

"Separate?"

She watched him digest the word as if it were a particularly tough piece of steak.

"We are not carting this baby back and forth between the two of us, Lilly."

"What are you suggesting, then?" she demanded flippantly. "That we stay together and live happily ever after?"

His lips curved in a smile that showed his teeth. "That's exactly what I'm suggesting, *tesoro*. Glad you're keeping up with me."

A feeling akin to shock settled over her. She studied his face, searching for some sign he was joking, but other than his twisted smile there was nothing but grim determination. Her chin lifted. "There is no way in hell I'm staying in an unhappy marriage. I know what it's like to grow up like that, and I won't do it to a child."

"You think it's better to subject them to a tug of war between two adults?"

"I think it's better to create an amicable separation where we both have this baby's best interests at heart."

"*Buona prova,* Lilly," he drawled. "But I'm not about to let your baggage destroy the future of our child. You contest this and I'll make it a court battle of epic porportions."

She shrugged out of his hold. "You are crazy. *This* is crazy." She looked at him desperately. "It will never work."

"It will work because we'll make it work." He crossed his arms over his chest and stood looking down at her like the impenetrable force he was. "Haven't we proved the last few weeks we can compromise?"

"About our social schedule," she said dully. How would a child fare in a marriage based solely on sex? In a marriage so far gone there was no pulling it back?

He lifted her chin with his fingers. "We have been good together lately, Lil. And we once had a fantastic marriage. We can make this work."

Or the bitterness between them would consume both them *and* their child, just as it had her.

She went for the jugular. "Don't you remember what it was like to live as part of a business partnership? Do you want that for yourself? For your child?"

"If what we've been doing in bed is a business partnership, then I'm all for it," he returned with a mocking smile. "Sign me up."

"You are—" She spun away, frustration burning a path of fire through her.

"A man who wants the family that was promised to

him," he rasped. "You are having my child, Lilly. De Campos don't divorce. So this is it. And I want more than one. My brothers are the most precious thing I have. I want that for our child."

Once she would have been sure he would say *she* was the most precious thing he had. Wrapping her arms around herself, she stared up at him. "So you were never going to let me walk away?"

"You would have been free to walk when our deal was up. But I would never have remarried."

Why? She wanted to scream it at him, but her throat felt as if it was closing over as the inevitability of what had happened hit her. How could she have been so stupid as to allow this to happen? To do the one thing that would bind her to the man she loved forever when she would never have his love back?

"I'm tired," she said abruptly, sure that if she attempted one more word she was going to sob. "I need some rest."

He let her go.

Overwhelmed and exhausted, she climbed the stairs to the bedroom, unzipped her dress and left it on the floor. She washed her face and brushed her teeth and slipped beneath the silk sheets of their bed. The dark, silent room finally allowed a refuge for her tears. They ran hot, silent, down her face.

What once would have been the news that completed her and Riccardo's dream had only driven them further apart.

She cried for that dream. She cried for her childhood. She cried for Riccardo's. She cried for the damage they had done to each other. And when he came after her and reached for her with strong, comforting hands she curled into him and let him hold her until her tears soaked his shirt.

"Don't be sad, *amore mio*," he murmured. "The past is the past. *We* are in control of our future and I promise you we can make this work."

My love. He'd said it not in the taunting tone he'd adopted of late, but the way he'd used to say it to her. Her sobs gradually subsided into big, hiccuping breaths that shook her body. When she was silent against him he undressed her and moved over her, kissing every inch of her skin. His passionate tenderness revealed more to her than he ever could have said with words.

They had a chance. He might not have meant the words literally—maybe they had just been to comfort her—but as her head rested on his chest and the solid warmth of him put her to sleep her heart told her differently. She had seen that look on his face before.

He cared more than he was saying.

Could she hope his feelings would eventually turn into love again, for the sake of their unborn child? Or was she just fooling herself in a very dangerous game?

CHAPTER ELEVEN

WHEN LILLY WAS a little girl she'd dreamed of attending a Hollywood movie premiere on the arm of a handsome man, with paparazzi flashbulbs exploding in her face as they made their way down the red carpet. She would blink, steady herself on his arm, and continue on, a big smile on her face as she showed off her very fabulous dress.

Never once, outside of those dreams, had she allowed herself to believe she would actually live that life. Not Lilly the awkward, shy farmgirl. Not even Lilly the graduate physiotherapist with a budding career in front of her, living in one of the most exciting cities in the world where red carpets were a star-studded fixture.

Then she'd met Riccardo. And her life had *become* that dream. Only for her to realize how lonely and empty a life it was.

She walked into her office and shut the door, feeling as if her life had come full circle. Tonight she was to walk the red carpet for the premiere of this summer's hottest blockbuster with her very own dark and dangerous male. The man she was falling more in love with every day she was with him.

She didn't want the dream. She wanted what was real. She wanted *him*.

She sank down in her office chair and dropped her head into her hands. She had married Riccardo for the man he'd been early in their marriage. And ever since they'd returned from Barbados she'd seen glimpses of him again.

He'd been by her side through all the doctor's appointments and tests, asking the pertinent questions her scrambled brain didn't think to. He'd made her sit down to a proper meal every night, and sent her to bed early. And when he did he would stay for a few minutes before he started working again. He would cradle her against him and talk to her, even confide in her if his mood was right. She was realizing how complex a man her husband was—that she'd never really *known* him in their two years of marriage.

Or one, if you counted the year they'd stopped talking.

He'd sacrificed so much for De Campo. And she was starting to see what becoming CEO would do for his soul. It was the final piece in the puzzle that was Riccardo De Campo.

She wondered how she'd never seen it before.

Weariness swept over her and she closed her eyes just for a moment. The weight of the decision she had to make was killing her. Was she going to follow her heart, agree to stay with Riccardo and hope she was right about his feelings for her? Or was she going to run and fight him all the way to the bitter end for custody of a child who would become a pawn in their tug of war?

She'd promised herself she would stop running. Which also meant running from herself.

She blinked to keep herself awake, so exhausted she wanted to crawl onto her desk and sleep there. She had nothing to wear tonight that fit, and hadn't had time to shop since she'd really started showing.

She wanted to walk the red carpet like she wanted a hole in her head.

But it was important to De Campo, this sponsorship, and she didn't really have a choice.

A knock sounded on the door. She pulled herself up off

her desk, expecting to see Katy. Instead Riccardo strolled through the door, looking as if he'd just slayed ten dragons and was ready to move on to the next. The smile on his face faded into a frown when he saw her wipe a trail of drool from the corner of her mouth.

"*Dio,* Lilly, you're sleeping at your *desk?*"

"Resting," she corrected, sitting up straight and smoothing her hair. "Wasn't I meeting you at home?"

"My meetings were canceled this afternoon." He walked over to her desk and leaned against the edge of it, his gaze resting on hers. "This is ridiculous. You're asleep on your feet."

"I'm fine," she murmured, standing up. "Just give me a minute to gather my stuff."

He waved her on. She shoved a file she was working on in her briefcase, along with the antacids that had become a new food group for her, and went to retrieve her sweater off the coat rack near the door.

"Jim—Riccardo here."

She turned to see her husband on his phone.

"Lilly and I can't make it to the premiere tonight. Can you and your wife attend in our place?"

Her eyes widened. She waved at him to say she was fine, but he held up a hand.

"Great. We'll drop off the tickets on our way home."

She stared at him as he disconnected the call. "I can't believe you just did that."

He lifted his shoulders. "Jim's the head of North American sales… It'll be a great networking opportunity for him."

"I would have been fine."

He crossed over to her. "I know you would have. You've been a trooper, *tesoro.* But enough's enough. I'm worried about you."

She pushed her hair out of her face. "It just hit me how tired I am."

"You're not getting enough rest." He ran his fingers down her cheek. "You have big black bags under your eyes."

"Heartburn," she lied. "But I am glad you canceled."

"Because you have nothing to wear?" His dark gaze slashed over her in a reprimand. "You refuse to go buy new clothes, because that would be admitting you're gaining weight, and you don't like the way you look. So I went out and bought some for you."

Her jaw dropped. "You mean you had Paige get me a dress for tonight?"

"No, *I* bought you a dress for tonight—plus the rest of the wardrobe you need." He shrugged. "I'm sure I forgot something, but it's a start."

"You went shopping?"

His teeth flashed white. "I run one of the world's top ten beverage companies, *cara*. A trip to a recommended fashion house isn't beyond my means."

She couldn't believe what she was hearing. "How did you know my size?"

He lifted his hands. "I told them you were this tall and like this." He arced his hands in the shape of an hourglass.

"You did?"

"I did. It's all in the car." He looked supremely satisfied with himself as he took her sweater and pushed her out the door in front of him. "I think I have pretty good taste."

He had exquisite taste. In everything. Lilly stared at the cream silk sweater draped over her arm. It was exactly the right size and style she would have chosen. As were the T-shirts, blouses, jeans and gowns he'd picked out.

He had forgotten nothing.

A lump the size of Mount Everest formed in her throat. The little pieces of her heart she'd thought shattered forever started to put themselves back together again.

His attention to detail wasn't surprising. What got her

was how in tune a big, macho man like him could be with what she loved. Who she was.

She pulled the last couple of items out of the bag—a sexy lilac-colored silk nightie she was sure Riccardo had chosen with himself in mind, and a pair of yoga pants. Fuchsia yoga pants. Her mouth twisted in her first real smile of the day.

She slipped her too-tight pants off and pulled on the pink pair. And sighed. To be in something that fit, that didn't make her feel like an overstuffed sausage, was heavenly. She added a T-shirt, pulled her hair into a ponytail, and went downstairs to find Riccardo.

She found him in the den—a cozy, comfortable room that housed their big screen TV and library.

"I ordered us Chinese," he told her. "Should be here in a few minutes."

"I've decided you are always to shop for me," she murmured, moving toward him. Lifting on tiptoe, she brushed a kiss across the light stubble that dusted his cheek. "Since you do such a good job."

He slid his arms around her waist. "I closed my eyes when I handed the woman the yoga pants."

"You get bonus points for those," she murmured, lifting her chin and inviting his kiss. She was rewarded with a hard, possessive one that left her breathless.

"You need to cut down on your schedule."

"I'm not taking any new patients. It'll gradually lessen."

He pressed his lips together, consciously controlling his automatic response, which she was sure would have been, *Cut it down now.*

"You also have to accept the changes in your body. They're natural and healthy."

"I'm getting there," she murmured. "It's just hard when it feels like my body is out of control. The control part is the hardest for me."

He spread his hands wide. "Just hand it over to me, *cara,* and I'll take care of it for you."

She made a face at him. "You would love that, wouldn't you?"

He caught her hand in his much larger one, the teasing light in his eyes darkening into seriousness. "No more keeping things inside, Lil. If you're struggling you need to tell me."

"I will. I promise."

He put some classical music on—a haunting piece of Mozart she knew was his favorite—then pulled her into his arms on the sofa while they waited for the food. She closed her eyes and rested her head against his chest. *This* was what she'd always wanted. The way they were when they were together like this.

At that moment she knew with certainty that everything he'd been holding back, everything he hadn't said to her these past few weeks, had been because she'd hurt him so badly. Because she'd deserted him when he'd needed her the most.

Because she had failed him.

"Ric?"

He pressed his lips to her hair. "Mmm?"

"I'm sorry for walking out on you. I'm sorry I gave up on us."

He stiffened. Then his arms tightened around her. For a long moment silence bound them together, her husky admission sitting on the air between them. Then he bent and pressed a kiss to her shoulder. "I've made so many mistakes too," he said thickly. "It wasn't just you."

Her eyes burned. Her throat was clogged with so much pent-up emotion she wasn't sure she could articulate it all. "I hurt you."

He turned her around so their gazes met. "We hurt each other."

"I want to make this work." Her voice came out husky, edged with the fear she felt.

His eyes were razor-sharp. "What do you mean?"

She sucked in a shuddering breath. "I was so angry with you at first—threatening to turn this into a custody battle, not giving me any choice in the matter. But then I realized you were right. It's time for me—for *us*—to move on. To let go of the past. To give this marriage the shot it deserves. To give our *baby* the home it deserves."

An emotion she wished desperately she could identify flashed in his eyes. He lifted his hands to frame her face.

"But I want *you,* Riccardo," she said shakily. "I don't want the Golden Man from the Golden Couple. I want the Riccardo De Campo who charmed me out of my phone number in that bar. The man who just wanted to be with me."

His gaze darkened to midnight. "You will have him," he promised huskily. "You have always been the only woman for me."

"You won't want me in a few months," she murmured. "I'll be so far from the woman you married you'll be repelled by me."

A smile curved his lips. "Don't you know there's nothing you could ever do to make me want you less? You're like a fire in my blood, *cara.* I want you all the time."

The heat in his eyes stole her breath. The reverence of his hands as he slipped her T-shirt over her head and cupped her breasts in his palms made it catch in her throat. And when he stripped the bra from her and set his mouth to her flesh she moaned her appreciation.

The pink yoga pants went next, landing on the floor in a heap. "This part you hate so much," he whispered, sliding his hands up over her hips, "allows you to carry my baby. And *that* is a miracle."

Her heart turned over and emotion so sharp it was almost painful sliced through her. When he was touching her, when he was holding her like this, his reverence eclipsed her insecurities and made her feel like the most beautiful woman on the planet.

She got the buttons undone on his shirt, divested him of his jeans and boxers, and then there was only his magnificent body, free for her to touch at will. She dropped to her knees and worshipped him, moved her lips over his perfect chest, his powerful abs, then down over the hard, throbbing length of him that telegraphed his desire for her. Reveling in his sharp intake of breath, she teased him until he begged—begged for her to take him into the heat of her mouth—and then, when he'd had all he could take of that, he begged for her to end the torture.

She crawled up his body and hooked her legs around his waist. Slowly, torturously, she took him inside her, prolonging it until sweat beaded on his forehead and he cursed out loud.

Her gaze locked with his. She wanted to look away, *needed* to look away, because surely her love for him was written across her face. But she'd promised honesty. To herself and to him. She kept her eyes on his as he allowed her to drive him crazy with shallow, then deeper twists of her hips. His eyes were closed. His big body was shaking with need. She had control. But she knew it was an illusion. She was about to take the biggest risk of her life. Bigger even than that day when she and Alex had driven out of Iowa, a dust cloud rising up behind the beat-up old car they'd paid a hundred dollars for, which had barely been moving, with nothing but hope and determination in their hearts.

He could cheat on her again. He could actually cheat this time. And there was nothing she could do but believe he would never do it. And she did. Because he was the only man who could turn her world from dark to light.

She could only hope that this didn't turn out to be her biggest mistake. That once he saw the messy, frightened truth of her he didn't run in the opposite direction.

Pleasure coursed through her, wave after wave, as his body swelled inside her, making it impossible to think. To worry. She closed her eyes and rocked her hips and took him over the edge. And let go of everything except her love for him.

CHAPTER TWELVE

THE DEEP TIMBRE of male voices greeted Lilly as she let herself into the townhouse. Her husband's smooth, rich baritone slid down her spine in a delicious reminder of how he'd woken her up this morning. A husky prompt to get out of bed, her own teasing reply, then a spark that burst into a flame that put both of them fifteen minutes behind schedule.

She kicked off her shoes. She was happy—so happy she felt as if she was floating on air. As if she'd figured out the secret of life.

Gabe's voice floated in from the terrace. A male with a deeper, more heavily accented tone responded. *Antonio?*

A twinge of disappointment sliced through her. She'd been hoping for another quiet night at home with Riccardo. Tonight she'd intended on telling him about Lisbeth. She couldn't hold off any longer because she was to fly to Switzerland in a couple of weeks. Finally she felt sure enough of what she and Riccardo had to tell him.

She was making peace with the past. She'd gone home for her mother's birthday a week ago. It hadn't been perfect. But it was progress. And now she would wipe any remaining secrets from her and Riccardo's relationship.

She waved at Magda in the kitchen before joining the men on the terrace.

"Cara." Riccardo's dark eyes lit with pleasure. "You're just in time to celebrate with us."

She crossed to his side and smiled up at him. "Celebrate what?"

Antonio strolled over and pressed a kiss to her cheeks. "I've just told Riccardo I am backing him as the next CEO of De Campo."

Her gaze lifted to her husband's. A quiet gleam of satisfaction burned in his eyes.

"Congratulations," she murmured, reaching up to brush a kiss across his cheek.

His lifted brow told her she would do better than that later. She smiled and tamped down her anxiety at the confirmation of what she'd known was coming but had secretly been dreading.

They had just gotten themselves back on track. Now the craziness would begin.

"Content to tend your vines?" she teased Gabe, walking over to greet him.

He smiled that serious Gabe smile she loved and kissed her. "The most crucial job in the company—*si.*"

She laughed and drew back. "But of course."

"I intend to endorse Riccardo tomorrow at the board meeting," Antonio said, nodding at his son.

Her throat tightened. *It was all happening so quickly.*

She moved back to Riccardo's side and slipped an arm around his waist. He would make a far better leader for De Campo than Antonio had. He would inspire the best in those who worked for him without using fear or intimidation as a threat. And she—she would shine for him. Riccardo needed her by his side, needed her to be the softness when everything else was a million-dollar decision. And this time she would not let the pressure get to her. She had the tools in place to manage her stress.

The De Campo men stayed for dinner. Tonight there was no need for Gabe to be his usual buffer between Antonio and Riccardo. There was rare harmony at the table. And she wondered, moving her gaze over her handsome, quietly confident brother-in-law, what it must have been like always to be the peacekeeper—always to be second best. In any other company Gabe would have made a brilliant CEO. Instead he made brilliant wine.

And maybe that was all he wanted.

After dinner Antonio excused himself to make a call. Lilly checked with Magda about dessert, then slipped out onto the terrace to get a breath of fresh air. The summer night was on the chilly side and she wrapped her arms around herself and stared up at the sky. It was so rare to see stars in Manhattan that the smattering overhead held her attention.

"My son's about to become one of the most powerful men on the planet." Antonio stepped out of the shadows and slid his mobile phone into his pocket. "Are you ready for this, Lilly?"

She wrapped her arms tighter around herself. What was it about these De Campo men, always trying to intimidate her?

"You must think I can or you wouldn't have mandated our reconciliation."

"Scusi?"

She gave him a level look. "Your condition, Antonio, for throwing your weight behind Riccardo. I take it our reconciliation has cemented your choice?"

He lifted a brow. "The performance of the company dictated my choice."

"But you wanted us to reconcile?"

He shrugged. "You're good for my son. I've always thought you had an excellent grounding effect on him. But it had nothing to do with my decision."

Her brain spun in a confused circle. "But you made our reconciliation a condition for your support."

An amused look spread across his face. "If Riccardo

said that he was using it as a way to get you back. You must know my son by now… He is solely focused on getting what he wants and damn the consequences."

She felt the blood drain from her face. Either Antonio or Riccardo was lying.

She prayed it was her father-in-law.

An icy numbness spread through her limbs. She lifted trembling hands to her face. "I—I think I'm going to go back inside. It's getting chilly out here."

She was halfway across the patio when Antonio's voice stopped her. "You look upset—but why? Riccardo may be ruthless in going after what he wants, *mia cara,* but is it so bad if he loves you that much?"

It *was* bad if he had lied to her without compunction. If he had preyed upon her in a moment of weakness, dangling a divorce in front of her she now wasn't sure he'd ever intended to give her.

"De Campos don't divorce."

He had never intended to let her go.

She excused herself from dessert, uncaring of her husband's concerned glance, sweeping upstairs before he had a chance to press her. She immersed her three and a half months pregnant body in a hot bath, desperate for something to soothe her. Desperate not to believe the man she had fallen in love with all over again could have lied to her like that when he had demanded honesty from *her.*

Damn him. She struggled to come up with a reason, an alternative explanation for why he'd done what he'd done. But there weren't any. There was nothing that excused what he'd done.

She closed her eyes and let the steaming water attack the numbness that had consumed her. Riccardo hadn't technically lied when he had talked about what had happened with Chelsea Tate. But it had been a lie by omission. And now he had lied again.

It was crazy. She'd *wanted* him to want her that much.

She'd *wanted* him to do exactly as she'd fantasized in the limo the night of their divorce party. To ride down her street on a white horse, climb through her window and carry her home.

But now she was afraid he was still the same old Riccardo, just cloaked in a new suit. The Riccardo who would use any weapon at his disposal to get what he wanted.

No. She slapped her hand against the water, sending bubbles flying. He had stood there on that terrace in Barbados and sworn to her they were going to create a marriage based on honesty and trust. And she had eaten it up like the naive Iowa farm girl she obviously still was.

Her insides crumbled. She'd made herself completely vulnerable to him. She had trusted him with her darkest secrets, trusted him to take care of her and their baby. And he had violated that trust.

Just like with everything else in her past—every time her parents' relationship had gone through a good patch and they'd actually been happy together, every time the farm had gone into the black and she'd been able to buy a new dress, or that bittersweet moment in Westchester when she'd thought she had everything she'd ever wanted—this brief moment of happiness had been taken from her. Just as she'd feared it would be.

She didn't know what was real anymore.

The moment he entered the room she sensed him. The air thickened around her. His grim appraisal as she opened her eyes made her sink further under the water.

"What's going on, Lilly?"

She swallowed past the lump in her throat. "You promised me honesty. You promised we could trust each other."

He nodded, his dark gaze fixed intently on her. "*Si.* Have I given you any reason to doubt me?"

She sat up and reached for the sides of the tub with shaking hands. "You *lied* to me, Riccardo. You lied to me about this whole crazy deal."

He paled. "What did Antonio say to you?"

"That you're a selfish bastard who'll do whatever it takes to get what you want." She stood up and jabbed a finger at him. "I trusted you. You told me we were starting over without any lies between us."

He took a step toward her. "I might have taken some artistic liberty with my wording, but Antonio *did* want us back together."

"You told me Antonio's support *depended* on us getting back together." She was shaking so hard she could hardly get the words out. "It was a bold-faced lie."

"What was I supposed to do?" he shot back tightly. "You wouldn't see me, you wouldn't talk to me, but you knew I wasn't going to give up."

Heat blazed through her. "You were supposed to *woo* me. You were supposed to come sit on my doorstep every night for a week, like you did when we first started dating. You were not supposed to *coerce* me into a reconciliation."

She stood there shivering violently. He grasped her wrists and pulled her out of the tub, wrapped a towel around her.

"Wooing wasn't working."

"The deal was a lie," she said dully. "And the only reason I accepted it was because of Lisbeth."

"Lisbeth?"

"Her leukemia is back. She needed treatment and I needed the money. So I agreed to your deal."

His expression darkened. "You agreed to reconcile with me because Lisbeth needed treatment? *Hell,* Lilly, what kind of a monster do you think I am that I wouldn't have given you that money if you'd told me?"

"I didn't want to be beholden to you. I didn't trust you. And look—" she threw her hands up in the air "—guess I was right."

His mouth flattened into a thin line, the nostrils of his Roman nose flaring. "You accuse *me* of not being com-

pletely honest when you are withholding things like that
from me?"

"It has nothing to do with us."

"It has *everything* to do with us. We are a family, Lilly.
We support each other."

"Well, now you've got your family," she bit out, feeling
her world fall apart. "Wife, baby—you've got everything
you ever wanted, just like you always do."

He closed his eyes, his long dark lashes sweeping down
over his cheeks. "It was never about that," he denied huskily. "I swear to you—it was never about that. I was—I was
desperately in love with you, Lilly, and I needed you back."

Her heart stopped. She took a deep breath, forcing herself to breathe, forcing her heart to start again—because
surely he would not use that tactic on her now. Not after
she'd spent weeks desperate to hear him say it.

She pulled the towel tight around her, fingers clenching the material. "How many other things have you lied
to me about?"

"Nothing." His voice vibrated with emotion. "Lilly—"

She held up a hand. "No more."

He ignored her and pulled her into his arms. The
strength and breadth of him dwarfed her, so achingly familiar she wanted to howl at the want in her.

His gaze bored into hers. "You are not a possession. You
and this baby we are going to have are the most precious
things in my life. How could I have let myself lose you? I
couldn't let that happen."

Hot tears escaped her eyes, running down her cheeks
like a river of fire. She beat her hands against his chest,
desperate for him to hurt as much as she was hurting. "I
needed this to be real. I needed *us* to be real this time."

"We are. Lilly—"

"No." She wrenched herself out of his arms, the towel
falling into a heap on the floor. "You know what Alex said
to me before we left for Barbados? 'Whatever you do, don't

get pregnant…' Because that was the one thing that would complicate a relationship that didn't need complicating." She closed her eyes. "And what do I do? I let exactly that happen. And *now* look at us."

He eyed her wild, naked stance apprehensively, as if she were a keg of dynamite poised to go off. "Let's get some clothes on you," he suggested quietly, "and then we'll talk."

She stalked past him into the bedroom and reached for the first piece of clothing she could lay her hands on. He followed, watching as she pulled on a T-shirt and jeans.

"Listen, I know you're emotional, *cara,* but—"

"I am not emotional." She wrenched her hair from underneath her T-shirt and whipped to face him. "I am crushed and I am saddened and I am *disappointed* in you. But I am *not* hormonal."

If she sounded insane she was past caring. "I need some time to myself," she muttered, turning back to search for a sweater. "Away from here. Away from you."

"You are not running away again."

"You're right." She swiped a sweater off a chair and shoved her arm in a sleeve. "I'm walking. Maybe to the Brooklyn Bridge. Who knows?"

He moved forward, took her by the shoulders and spun her around. His eyes were black, stormy. "You can throw away a million rings and I will still come after you."

She squared her shoulders. "I need time. Do not follow me. Don't have anyone follow me, for that matter. Or I swear to God you'll push me over the edge."

She turned and walked out the door. The stars were still shining brightly when she climbed into Riccardo's Jag and reversed it down the driveway. But this time she didn't look up.

CHAPTER THIRTEEN

RICCARDO KNOTTED HIS tie with fingers that weren't quite steady. This should have been the most important day of his life—the day his father anointed him the new head of De Campo. It should have been the crowning glory of three years spent proving to Antonio that he had what it took—that this was *his* company and his vision was the future. That the passion in his veins ran as deep as it did through his father's.

But his wife was gone. His *pregnant* wife was gone. And he had no idea where she was, what her state of mind was, or what he was supposed to do with the unfamiliar feeling of helplessness pulsing through him. Giving a speech to the board that painted a vision of De Campo's future seemed inconceivable.

His hands dropped away from his tie. Lilly had made it clear she needed space. If he had denied it to her, gone after her, he would have lost her.

If he hadn't already.

He shrugged on his jacket, lifted his collar clear of the dark gray Armani that was his good luck suit—the suit he'd been wearing the night he'd met Lilly in that bar—and refused even to contemplate the possibility. Instead he thought about the twists and turns life could take. Antonio had wanted to raise racehorses. He'd ended up with vines and a company that had brought him success beyond his wildest dreams. Motor racing had been *his* passion, but he'd grown to love the business that was bigger than him, bigger than his brothers and his father now. De Campo had come to signify luxury and refinement on a global scale. It was bigger than all of them. He would be the man who took it to new heights. Who exploited its raw potential.

Sometimes things happened that were beyond your control.

Sometimes you made them happen with your own arrogance and stupidity.

He stared at his reflection in the mirror, searching for some sign of life in his perfectly tailored appearance. A machine stared back at him. None of this meant anything without Lilly. He could handle the dull throb he woke with every day he wasn't racing as long as she was by his side. But he could not fathom the future without her.

His chest ached with the need to have his wife back.

Shaking it off—shaking it off because he had to—he straightened his shoulders and went downstairs to where Tony was waiting with the car. His longtime driver said hello, gave him a quick look, and eliminated his usual witty banter.

Riccardo slid into the backseat and pressed his head against the leather. He'd felt justified in coercing Lilly into the deal because it had been the only weapon he'd had against her refusal to see him. Because he loved her. He was so used to having to fight tooth and nail to get what he wanted from Antonio he'd carried that same demeanor into his personal life. Strategize and conquer. But with all of his and Lilly's trust issues he should have known better. He should have at least come clean when he'd had the chance to in Barbados.

Muddled thinking from a man who had seen the destructive effects of secrets harbored.

He clasped his hands together in his lap and looked down at the gleaming gold wedding band Lilly had placed on his finger. He'd been forgiven once. Would he be forgiven again? Or had he made one mistake too many?

The urge to put his fist through the bulletproof window overwhelmingly strong, he switched his attention to the traffic on Fifth Avenue instead, curling his fist on his lap. Lilly had called in to her clinic to say she wouldn't be in. After she hadn't picked up her cell he'd called Alex, to see if she was with her. Which had, in turn, opened him up to her sister's sarcastic demand to know what he'd done *now*.

He ran a hand over his chin, his uneven shaving job making him frown. Where in *Dio's* name was she? And why wouldn't she at least pick up the phone and let him know she was okay?

Paige handed him a stack of messages when he walked in. He crumpled them up and threw them on his desk.

"Everyone's here," she murmured, moving her gaze from the wad of paper back to him. "You okay?"

Did he *look* okay? He gave her a curt nod, dropped his briefcase by his desk and took his laptop out.

His father gave him a nod as he walked into the boardroom. *"Siete pronti?"*

"Pronto." Ready.

Gabe took the chair beside him. "You look like hell, *fratello.* Too much champagne last night?"

"I can't find Lilly."

His brother blinked. *"Scusi?"*

He powered up his laptop. "We had a fight last night and she needed some space."

"You have no idea where she went?"

"None." His jammed his palm against the table. She was pregnant. Driving his far too powerful car. And emotional.

Antonio opened the meeting and ran through the agenda. Riccardo looked down at the notes for his speech. There were only five words on the cue card. *Vision. Courage. Expertise. Timing. Domination.* They would define De Campo's future.

His father began his pitch to endorse his son as CEO. Riccardo checked his messages on his phone. *Nothing.*

"As you have seen over the past three years, my son Riccardo has transformed De Campo into the multifaceted global brand that it is today…"

Antonio's voice droned on, blurred into nothingness. It was only when his father turned to him and put his hands together, and the board followed suit, that he realized it was time.

"I am throwing my full support behind Riccardo De Campo for the position of CEO of this company."

The board members stood and clapped.

It was happening.

This time as he made his way to the podium and shook Antonio's hand there was no mistaking the pride gleaming in his father's eyes. He felt strong and weak at the same time—as if he was both that boy who'd trailed after his father into the vineyard asking a million questions and the man he'd become.

He cleared his throat and stepped to the microphone.

"For the last three years I have watched the De Campo Group grow from a fledgling global brand to a force to be reckoned with in the industry. We gambled. Our vision was big. Our vision was ambitious. But our vision was right." He paused and cast his gaze around the room. "And now we sit poised on a precipice. We can either move with the future or we can lose our way, as so many other brands have done. I say we move—that we have the guts and the vision to—"

Paige stepped into the back of the room. It was highly unusual for her to interrupt a meeting of this importance, and the look on her face stopped him cold.

Lilly. He knew it as instinctively as he knew the sun rose in the east.

"Excuse me." He stepped down from the podium and walked toward the back of the room. Antonio frowned and stood up as he passed. The buzzing in his ears got louder the closer he got to Paige. Her eyes were glued to his face and she stood wringing her hands together—something his PA never did.

Antonio announced they would take a quick break.

"I have Lilly on the line," Paige whispered to him. "Riccardo, she doesn't sound good."

He sprinted to Paige's desk and picked up the line. *"Lilly?"*

"Riccardo?"

"Yes," he barked. Her voice was faint. Not right. "Lilly, where are you?"

"I—I'm not feeling well. Ric, I—"

"Lilly?"

The line went dead. He slammed the receiver down and stood staring at it.

Paige's hand flew to her mouth. "She said her phone was dying."

He was already halfway into his office. "Call the security company and have her phone traced. *Now.* I need to know where she is."

Antonio and Gabe joined him in his office.

"What the hell are you doing?" his father demanded. "They're waiting to hear from you."

"There's something wrong with Lilly," he said grimly. "I've got to find her."

Antonio gave him an incredulous look. "Surely it can wait fifteen minutes?"

"No, it can't!" Riccardo roared. "Gabe, I need your keys."

His brother dug them out of his pocket. "I'll come with you."

"You should stay here and hold down the fort."

"I'm not sure you should—"

He ripped the keys out of his brother's hand. "I'll call when I know something."

Mid-morning traffic was still thick. He crawled forward, trying not to think about how weak and scared Lilly had sounded. Why had he let her go last night?

Paige called. Lilly had last been tracked in Westchester. *She was at the house.* He changed lanes and headed for the interstate, relieved, and then his heart started to pound as all sorts of disturbing images crammed his head. What if something was wrong with her pregnancy? The house was on the water. What if she'd taken one of the boats out and started to feel ill? Or gotten weak while swimming?

What if she was lying somewhere helpless?

He put his foot down on the accelerator and gunned the Maserati, weaving in and out of traffic as if he was in the Monaco Grand Prix. When he hit the interstate he put the pedal to the floor. The powerful car ate up the miles, but it wasn't fast enough. Not for the torturous images running through his head.

The guy in front of him was driving like his grandmother in the left lane. He jammed his foot on the accelerator and sent the car to twice the legal speed limit, passing him on the inside.

The sirens started ten minutes out of Westchester. Red flashing lights blazed in his rearview mirror. For a split second he contemplated ignoring them. He could outdrive them in this car, he knew. But the whir of a helicopter overhead convinced him the cop on the ground wasn't the only one after him.

He slowed down and pulled onto the side of the road. The cop pulled in behind him and got out of his car. He'd just explain what was going on and then he'd be on his way...

A tall, beefy cop stopped by his window. "License and registration."

Riccardo handed it to him. "Officer—I—"

"Do you have any idea how fast you were going, sir?"

"About a hundred. But, Officer, I—"

The cop jabbed a finger at him. "You, sir, are a dangerous driver. You aren't walking away with this car today. I can tell you that."

"Look, I—"

The officer looked at his license and started to laugh. "You're kidding me? Riccardo De Campo the racecar driver?"

"Former racecar driver," Riccardo corrected. "I can explain why I was driving so fast. My—"

"Save it. You're not the first superstar to think you can flaunt the rules."

"*Officer!*" Riccardo yelled. "My wife is sick. She's pregnant. I was racing to get to her."

The cop blinked. "Where?"

"Our Westchester house. It's ten minutes from here."

"Did you call an ambulance?"

He closed his eyes. "No." *Why hadn't he?*

The cop gave him a considering look. "You better be telling the truth."

"I am," Riccardo rasped desperately. "Can I go?"

"You will follow me," the cop said sternly. "You so much as step one inch out of line and I will impound both you *and* your car."

Riccardo nodded and gave him directions. The cop put on his siren and thankfully was no slouch in the speed department either, getting them to the house in just under fifteen minutes.

He found Lilly in the living room, lying on the sofa.

"Cara." He dropped down on his knees beside her. She was curled in the fetal position, her face about five shades paler than it normally was.

"I didn't mean to scare you," she murmured. "The phones here aren't working and my cell phone died."

"They've been working on the lines out here. Lil—" He took her hands in his. "Can you tell me what doesn't feel right?"

She bit her lip. "I don't know. I—I'm nauseous and I'm having bad pains."

Riccardo looked up at the cop, who'd come in behind him, but the officer was already on his radio, calling for an ambulance.

A tear rolled down her cheek. "I didn't want to bother you. You had that meeting…"

He gripped her hands tighter. "I don't care if I'm having lunch with the Pope. You need me—you call me."

A river of tears ran down her cheeks.

"Are the pains getting worse or better?"

"Worse. There's more of them now."

His insides went cold. "When did they start?"

"A couple hours ago." She closed her eyes as a tremor ran through her slim body. "Ric—something's wrong. I don't feel right."

He sat down and pulled her into his arms. "It's going to be all right, *tesoro,* I promise you. The ambulance is on its way."

She burrowed into him. The tension in her body made his own stiffen with fear.

"I'm so sorry. You should be in that meeting, and if I screw up your ch—"

"Ssh." He pressed a kiss against her hair. "You're the most important thing in the world to me, Lilly."

"Yes, but the job is—"

He pressed his fingers to her mouth. "The job is nothing without you. *I* am nothing without you. Haven't you realized that yet? I do these stupid things because I love you. Because I can't bear the thought of losing you."

Her lashes fluttered down over those beautiful hazel eyes. "I spent the morning walking along the river, thinking."

His heart jammed in his chest.

The tears streamed harder down her face now, running

over the edge of her chin. "I love you, Riccardo. I've never stopped loving you. Not even for a minute."

He felt as if the sun had come out on this dreary, overcast summer day. The flash of joy that swept through him was powerful. Followed by sick, overwhelming relief that he hadn't lost her.

"Please forgive me," he whispered. "That was my last big mistake. Ever."

She shook her head. "It was my running too. I can see that now. I was so scared that once you saw the truth of me—how messed up I am still—you wouldn't want me anymore."

He brought her hand to his mouth and pressed his lips to her knuckles. "We all have our baggage, *cara*. Look what you've done with your life. You help little boys walk again. Nothing I've ever done comes close to that."

Her eyes glittered with an emotion that stole his breath.

"We have to be honest with each other. No more lies. No matter how little or how painful the truth."

"Agreed." He held her tightly as another shudder racked her body and glanced up at the cop. The officer held up two fingers.

"I mean it." Lilly bumped her hand against his chest. "Three strikes and you're out, Riccardo De Campo."

"Then it's a good thing I don't need anymore," he murmured. "*You* are all I need."

"Ambulance is here." The cop abandoned his post at the window. "Let's go."

Riccardo picked up Lilly and strode outside. She was going to be fine. She *had* to be fine. There was no other way to think.

CHAPTER FOURTEEN

THE GRAY-HAIRED emergency room physician walked into the waiting room where Riccardo, Gabe, Alex and—surprisingly—Antonio, who'd shown up a couple of hours ago sat, just over three hours after they'd taken Lilly in. He wore the unsmiling, grim look of a man who'd been working too many hours straight.

Riccardo's heart dropped to the floor.

The elderly physician stopped in front of him, a tired smile curving his mouth. "They're both fine. Lilly's suffering from pre-eclampsia—a high blood pressure condition associated with pregnancy. Very common, but she'll need to see her doctor often."

His shoulders sagged with relief. "And the pain?"

"Under control. You can take her home as soon as we can do the paperwork, but you'll need to schedule an appointment with her obstetrician as soon as possible. Get some more detailed tests done."

He released the breath he'd been holding in a long, heavy exhale. *Lilly was fine. Their baby was fine.*

Thank God.

The doctor smiled. "Glad I could give out some good news today. There hasn't been a surplus of it."

"*Grazie,*" he murmured huskily. "I can't say it enough."

The doctor waved him off and headed back into the chaos. Alex went in and spent a few minutes with her sister before Riccardo took her home. Gabe went to get him a cup of coffee for the ride.

He rested his elbows on his thighs and dropped his head into his hands. Moisture stung the backs of his eyes, mixing with a relief so profound it was all-consuming.

A hand gripped his shoulder. "Your mother suffered from pre-eclampsia. Lilly will be fine."

He looked up at Antonio through glazed eyes. He'd been shocked when his father had arrived and waited with them without a word. The emotion darkening his father's silver eyes shocked him even more.

Antonio straightened, as if the show of affection had thrown him off balance. "You don't need to worry about the board," he said roughly. "I made sure you have a hundred and ten percent of their support."

Riccardo held his gaze for a long moment. *"Grazie."*

He had Lilly. Now he could think about the future.

Lilly prided herself on the toughness at her core. It had carried her out of Iowa and into a life she could only have dreamed of. It had helped her give that same strength to her patients when they were intent on giving up. But the vulnerability she felt walking toward the front door of the hospital was so soul-searing it was hard to keep walking in a straight line.

A nurse pushed the door open for her and she walked out into the light drizzle to Riccardo, waiting with the car at the curb. Her legs trembled as her husband walked toward her—tall, imposing, with a determined set to his mouth that made her want to fling herself into his arms.

What if he hadn't come after her? What if she'd lost him?

Her knees wobbled as he took the last couple of steps and pulled her into his arms. She closed her eyes and absorbed his strength, that determination. It was enough for both of them.

"Let's go home," he said quietly.

They made the drive back to Manhattan in silence, an acknowledgement of what they'd almost lost heavy in the air. Riccardo held her hand in his lap the entire way, as if he couldn't bear to let her go.

Their stately old limestone townhouse awaited them—the scene of her rollercoaster marriage which had run from perfect to miserable to all she'd ever wanted. Majestic, it glimmered in the late-afternoon sunlight, so solid with its heavy brick façade it would stand forever.

She stepped out of the car, her mind traveling back to that night four and a half months before, when limos had lined up in this driveway to witness the destruction of her and Riccardo.

Tonight it was unusually quiet. There were no limos. No drivers chatting. No false illusions of perfection on either part. There was only the here and now and what they chose to do with it.

Riccardo came around the car and slid his arm around her waist. "What are you thinking?"

"We have a blank slate," she said huskily. "The story is ours to write."

He tugged her closer and lifted her chin with his fingers. "I predict a very happy ending."

She drank him in—the hard, strong lines of his face that could soften into devastating humor, the sensuous pull of his lips that could make her crazy for him. He loved her. He was crazy about her. That much she was sure of. And that was enough.

Her lips curved. "You think so, Signor De Campo?"

"I know so, Signora De Campo."

He swung her into his arms and carried her up the front walk.

For her and Riccardo this past year had been simply a twist in the road of a lifetime together.

And tomorrow was another day.

EPILOGUE

Westchester, New York

"I DON'T KNOW about you, but I think he needs a strong, manly name to match his personality."

"Papà."

One-and-a-half-year-old Marco ducked under Lilly's arm and ran as fast as his short, stumpy legs would carry him across the terrace to where her husband stood, indecently attractive in a navy pinstriped suit. Her heart contracted as her son flung himself around Riccardo's legs. The two males had a love affair going on that was a joy to watch.

She would normally have let herself drool a little longer over the suit that set off her husband's swarthy good looks to perfection, but the squirming bundle of fluff in his arms demanded her attention.

It looked suspiciously like a chocolate-brown Labrador Retriever puppy.

"*Cucciolo!*" Marco squealed, tugging on his father's pant leg. "*Giù,*" he ordered, in an imperious tone that was already so close to his father's Lilly was afraid he was going to skip the baby stage entirely and move straight to domination.

Riccardo bent and set the puppy on the ground. Marco

grabbed onto its fur so hard the puppy backed up and cowered against Riccardo's leg.

"*Dolcemente,*" her husband instructed, scooping the puppy up in one arm and Marco in the other. "You are a brute, Marco De Campo."

"Just like his daddy." Lilly sighed. "Well, most of the time anyway," she teased, standing up on tiptoe to kiss him. But between the squirming, licking puppy and the delighted Marco it was a pretty fruitless effort.

"Hold that thought," Riccardo murmured. "I have a surprise for you too, but you'll get it later."

Heat rose to her face.

He laughed—a low, sexy rumble that did jittery things to her insides. "*That* is a given, *tesoro.* But I also stumbled upon something else I thought you'd like."

Mortified that her thoughts always seemed to involve her husband and some sort of naked activity, she took the puppy from him and felt her heart melt at the tiny bundle of fur, the big brown eyes and giant paws. "I thought this was happening in the spring?"

He lifted his shoulders. "The breeder had someone cancel at the last minute. I made the mistake of going to see him, and well…"

She smiled as the puppy licked her face with boundless enthusiasm. "I wouldn't have been able to resist him either."

"His name's Dutch. But we can rename him."

She lifted a brow.

"Dutch chocolate?"

She hated it. "We'll rename."

"Thought so. You were about to swim?"

She nodded. "We didn't expect you for hours."

Her husband's gaze rested on her face with that singular intensity he devoted to everything he focused on. "I ducked out early. I missed you."

A lump formed in her throat. Her life was as close to perfect as a life could be. So perfect, in fact, that some days when it seemed *too* perfect, as if it could never last, she retreated to the back porch of the house here in Westchester, where they'd move for the summer, and stayed there until her heart stopped racing and the feeling went away. It was where Riccardo inevitably found her. And instinctively he'd always know what to say, because this beautiful, autocratic man who'd suffered plenty of his own heartaches knew her better than anyone.

He'd been there every step of the way.

She ran her fingers down the hard lines of his face. They still had their blow-outs—and, boy, were they blow-outs when they happened. That had never changed. But they were few and far between, and beneficial from the point of view that they both got their feelings out and moved on.

Marco scrunched up his face and shoved a beefy little hand against Riccardo's chest. "Swim. *Cucciolo.*"

Lilly laughed. "Maybe no swimming for the puppy today. But we can."

They splashed in the shallow end of the pool and Riccardo changed, then joined them. Lilly sat on the edge of the pool, dangling her legs in the water while her husband tossed Marco high. Her son's delighted yelps filled the air.

Her husband lifted a brow. "Enjoying your part-time life?"

"Oh, yes." She'd opted to cut back to part-time hours after Marco had been born, sharing her workload with another physiotherapist who also had a family. It allowed her to focus on work *and* her family, and she was loving every minute of it.

Marco slapped his hand on the water and sprayed water in Riccardo's face. Her lips curved. He was not only a solid little dark-haired mirror image of his father he was just as much of a daredevil. Fearless. Willing to try everything. Nothing like his mother had been like as a child. And she was glad for that.

Marco Alfonso De Campo. Named after Riccardo's racing hero and former teammate Marco Agostino, who'd died in a crash just weeks before their Marco had been born. His second name was after Riccardo's grandfather, who had built the first De Campo vineyard in Tuscany.

She blinked, her eyes stinging with the bittersweet emotion that seemed to define her life now. With the naming of Marco her husband seemed to have moved on, to have made amends with the past. He no longer shut down if racing came up. He acknowledged the subject, then moved on.

She had moved on too. It would never be a perfect relationship, but she was making strides with her parents. They were in love with Marco, and she visited a few times a year to give them a chance to spend time together. And somehow that was enough.

Riccardo caught her eye across the water. "Lisbeth's met an investment banker. She had stars in her eyes when he dropped her off the other night."

Oh, no. Of all the men in New York, investment bankers had to be the most arrogant. "Did you *do* something about it?"

A smile tugged at the corners of his mouth. "What was I supposed to do? Put the fear of God in him?"

"Yes. You should have." Her sister had been in remission for six months now. She'd come to live with them in New York after her treatment and was set to start college in the fall. She was so much like her former vibrant self it felt almost as if a miracle had happened, but Lilly was still fiercely protective of her. She was so vulnerable in so many ways.

But then again, she reminded herself, she'd been the same way when she'd moved to New York, and it had done her a world of good to stand on her own two feet in a city as tough as Manhattan.

"On second thought," she murmured, "maybe this is a good thing. She *should* have her heart broken a few times. It'll teach her how to deal with you alpha males."

His dark eyes glittered. "Maybe so. You've figured out how to have *this* one hopelessly within your power."

She glanced at him from beneath lowered lashes. "You think so?"

"Undoubtedly."

She put the heat in his gaze on hold while they enjoyed the afternoon, took care of the puppy, then fed and put their son to bed. Riccardo read to Marco while she changed. Her soft, cream-colored jersey dress that showed an ample amount of cleavage was meant to put his theory to the test. Her husband's deep velvet stare as she walked out onto the terrace gave her the answer she was looking for.

Just tamable enough.

He finished mixing their drinks. "New dress?"

"Yes."

"Come here."

Her heart went pitter-patter in her chest as she closed the distance between them. "What is *that?*" she questioned, staring at the murky dark liquid in the glass he handed her.

A satisfied smile touched his lips. "It so happens Lewis, our Bajan bartender friend, has become an international celebrity. The recipe for his house specialty has made it into one of the top food and beverage magazines."

"You're kidding?"

"Would I lie to you about something like that? He calls it his 'love potion'. The 'ultimate aphrodisiac.'"

An all-over body flush consumed her. *A love potion?* She could only think of three words. Hottest. Sex. Ever.

Riccardo read her expression. "Exactly," he drawled. "Drink up."

She took a sip. "Doesn't taste any better than I remember."

"It gets better the more you drink. Remember that?"

She sipped on the potent drink, wincing as the alcohol hit her empty stomach.

"What's that?" she asked, pointing at the tabloid he'd set on the bar. "I thought we weren't reading that stuff."

"You should read Jay Kaiken's column."

Ugh. "Really?"

"Yes. Read it."

She took another sip of her drink, thinking she might need it. Jay Kaiken's column was an account of the posh benefit she and Riccardo had attended for former super-model Gillian King's Manhattan clinic for eating disorders. A friend of Gillian's, Lilly had instantly seen the value of a place where women could go to be surrounded by those who were going through the same thing they were. And when Gillian had asked her to speak at the event she'd decided it was time for her to tell her story publicly. Even if it only helped one person, that was enough.

"Perhaps the most poignant moment of the evening was Lilly De Campo's account of her struggle with anorexia," Kaiken had written. *"Courageous and truthful, its honesty no doubt made an impression on everyone in attendance. I'm pretty sure there wasn't a dry eye in the crowd."* And, in true Kaiken tongue-in-cheek fashion, he'd added, *"PS—can I say how good it is to have the De Campos back together? I always did want to believe in fairytales…"*

She looked up at Riccardo, her vision blurring.

"It *was* very courageous of you," he said quietly. "But then again you're the most courageous woman I know, Lilly De Campo."

She stepped in to kiss him as she'd wanted to this afternoon. Heat swept through her veins, licked at her nerve-endings as he claimed her mouth in a thorough, possessive kiss that seemed to promise a million forevers.

"I love you," she whispered. *"Io ti amo per sempre."*

I will love you forever.

He pulled back, his gaze so dark it was almost black. "Finish that drink," he muttered roughly. "Dinner can wait."

She downed the last gulp and gasped when he swung her up in his arms and headed for the stairs. Up he climbed, to the bedroom that overlooked the river, the room where her dream of their family had begun. It occurred to her as Riccardo slid his hands to the back of her dress and unzipped it, letting the silky material slip to the floor, that her dream had finally come true. The puppy sleeping downstairs in a basket in the kitchen had been the final piece.

She smiled and wrapped her arms around her husband's neck, pulling his mouth down to hers.

From a divorce party to forever. Who would have known?

* * * * *

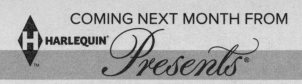

#3189 A DANGEROUS SOLACE
by Lucy Ellis
Gianluca Benedetti might not initially recognize Ava Lord, but the memories soon come rushing back! Exploring their reignited passion, Ava realizes the danger of opening her heart, as the closer he gets, the more cracks in her armor appear....

#3190 SECRETS OF A POWERFUL MAN
The Bond of Brothers
by Chantelle Shaw
Salvatore Castallano is haunted by the accident that left a blank in his memory. His young daughter is the one bright light in his dark existence. He'll do anything for her...even move Darcey Rivers—a delicious temptation—into his castle!

#3191 VISCONTI'S FORGOTTEN HEIR
by Elizabeth Power
Magenta is finally on track after suffering from amnesia. But, meeting Andreas Visconti's familiar gaze, she *knows* he's the father of her child! It's crucial she decipher the scattered puzzle of her mind and recall more than just memories of his touch....

#3192 A TOUCH OF TEMPTATION
The Sensational Stanton Sisters
by Tara Pammi
CEO Kimberly Stanton has rocked the international business world with the announcement of her marriage to outrageous Brazilian bad-boy tycoon Diego Pereira, *and* a pregnancy! If salacious rumors are already spreading, who can say what lies ahead for society's most notorious couple?

YOU CAN FIND MORE INFORMATION ON UPCOMING HARLEQUIN® TITLES, FREE EXCERPTS AND MORE AT WWW.HARLEQUIN.COM.

HPCNM1013RB

REQUEST YOUR FREE BOOKS!

2 FREE NOVELS PLUS
2 FREE GIFTS!

YES! Please send me 2 FREE Harlequin Presents® novels and my 2 FREE gifts (gifts are worth about $10). After receiving them, if I don't wish to receive any more books, I can return the shipping statement marked "cancel." If I don't cancel, I will receive 6 brand-new novels every month and be billed just $4.30 per book in the U.S. or $4.99 per book in Canada. That's a saving of at least 14% off the cover price! It's quite a bargain! Shipping and handling is just 50¢ per book in the U.S. and 75¢ per book in Canada.* I understand that accepting the 2 free books and gifts places me under no obligation to buy anything. I can always return a shipment and cancel at any time. Even if I never buy another book, the two free books and gifts are mine to keep forever.

106/306 HDN FVRK

Name _____ (PLEASE PRINT) _____

Address _____ Apt. #

City _____ State/Prov. _____ Zip/Postal Code _____

Signature (if under 18, a parent or guardian must sign)

Mail to the **Harlequin® Reader Service:**
IN U.S.A.: P.O. Box 1867, Buffalo, NY 14240-1867
IN CANADA: P.O. Box 609, Fort Erie, Ontario L2A 5X3

**Are you a current subscriber to Harlequin Presents books
and want to receive the larger-print edition?
Call 1-800-873-8635 or visit www.ReaderService.com.**

* Terms and prices subject to change without notice. Prices do not include applicable taxes. Sales tax applicable in N.Y. Canadian residents will be charged applicable taxes. Offer not valid in Quebec. This offer is limited to one order per household. Not valid for current subscribers to Harlequin Presents books. All orders subject to credit approval. Credit or debit balances in a customer's account(s) may be offset by any other outstanding balance owed by or to the customer. Please allow 4 to 6 weeks for delivery. Offer available while quantities last.

Your Privacy—The Harlequin® Reader Service is committed to protecting your privacy. Our Privacy Policy is available online at www.ReaderService.com or upon request from the Harlequin Reader Service.

We make a portion of our mailing list available to reputable third parties that offer products we believe may interest you. If you prefer that we not exchange your name with third parties, or if you wish to clarify or modify your communication preferences, please visit us at www.ReaderService.com/consumerschoice or write to us at Harlequin Reader Service Preference Service, P.O. Box 9062, Buffalo, NY 14269. Include your complete name and address.

HARLEQUIN®
Presents®

Jennie Lucas's latest story is packed full of
passion, power and so much more!

Don't miss

THE
CONSEQUENCES OF
THAT NIGHT

November 2013

An indecent indiscretion!

When one night with his housekeeper, Emma, has
serious consequences, billionaire Cesare Falconeri
must break his own vow—and say *I do* for the sake of
his heir. Now he'll expect his new bride to be *sharing*
his bed instead of making it!

www.Harlequin.com

HP13193